The Submission

by Jeff Talbott

SAMUEL FRENCH

FOUNDED 1830

SAMUELFRENCH.COM

ISBN 978-0-573-70043-9   Printed in U.S.A.   #20266

MUSIC USE NOTE

Licensees are solely responsible for obtaining formal written permission from copyright owners to use copyrighted music in the performance of this play and are strongly cautioned to do so. If no such permission is obtained by the licensee, then the licensee must use only original music that the licensee owns and controls. Licensees are solely responsible and liable for all music clearances and shall indemnify the copyright owners of the play and their licensing agent, Samuel French, Inc., against any costs, expenses, losses and liabilities arising from the use of music by licensees.

IMPORTANT BILLING AND CREDIT
REQUIREMENTS

All producers of *THE SUBMISSION* *must* give credit to the Author of the Play in all programs distributed in connection with performances of the Play, and in all instances in which the title of the Play appears for the purposes of advertising, publicizing or otherwise exploiting the Play and/or a production. The name of the Author *must* appear on a separate line on which no other name appears, immediately following the title and *must* appear in size of type not less than fifty percent of the size of the title type.

In addition the following credit *must* be given in all programs and publicity information distributed in association with this piece:

World Premiere at the MCC Theater, September 8, 2011
Artistic Directors: Robert Lupone, Bernard Telsey & William Cantler
Executive Director: Blake West

THE SUBMISSION received its world premiere at MCC Theater, opening September 27, 2011, at the Lucille Lortel Theater, in New York City, presented by artistic directors Robert LuPone, Bernard Telsey, and William Cantler, with set design by David Zinn, costume design by Anita Yavich, lighting design by David Weiner, music by Ryan Rumery and Christian Frederickson, sound design by Ryan Rumery, projections by Darrel Maloney, production management by B. D. White, production stage management by Timothy R. Semon, and general management by Ted Rounsaville. The director was Walter Bobbie. The cast was as follows:

DANNY	Jonathan Groff
TREVOR	Will Rogers
PETE	Eddie Kaye Thomas
EMILIE	Rutina Wesley

THE SUBMISSION was the winner of the 2011 Laurents/Hatcher Award for Best New Play.

THE SUBMISSION was the winner of the 2012 Outer Critics Circle John Gassner Award for a New American Play.

CHARACTERS

DANNY – 27. White.
TREVOR – 27. White.
PETE – 27. White.
EMILIE – 27. Black.

TIME

The play spans one year, September–September.

AUTHOR'S NOTES

The play is performed without an intermission.

Transitions into/out of scenes should be fast and punchy, lights snapping up full at top of scenes, snapping to black at the end; music (if used) should be percussive and sharp, possibly even abrasive; scenery should be minimal to make transitions short. Many of the scenes take place in a popular coffee chain. Unless otherwise indicated, each of these scenes is in a different location of the same chain; they look almost identical. Almost.

DANNY's script is always in sight.

A "(Beat.)" is like a rest in music; its length depends on what surrounds it. This is particularly true in the last scene (Scene 11).

With deep gratitude to Stephen Willems, Terrence McNally, Walter Bobbie, MCC Theater, The Laurents/Hatcher Foundation, Jonathan Lomma and Kenneth Jones, this play is dedicated to Arthur Laurents.

A great debt of thanks is owed to the following actors who gave their time and talent to the development of this play: of course the amazing Jonathan Groff, Will Rogers, Eddie Kaye Thomas and Rutina Wesley; and also Nathan Anderson, Kelli Colaco, Will Connell, Jessiee Datino, Michael Esper, Reg Flowers, Enid Graham, Brendan Griffin, Lucas Hall, Brad Heberlee, Robert Henry, Haskell King, Stephen Kunken, Zachary Quinto, Johnny Russell, Blaine Smith, Brian J. Smith, Jenn Thompson, Owen Thompson and Wayne Wilcox, with a note of particular thanks to Afton Williamson.

Scene 1

(A Coffee Chain)

*(September. Jackets, sweaters. **DANNY** and **TREVOR** sit at a table, several empty coffee cups around them. **DANNY** is typing on his laptop. **TREVOR** is reading loose pages of a script. **DANNY** stops to watch **TREVOR** reading, then goes back to typing. Beat. **DANNY** stops typing.)*

DANNY. Yo, muthahfuckah, are you–?

TREVOR. Shhh.

DANNY. OK.

*(Beat. **DANNY** types. **TREVOR** reads.)*

Are you almost–?

TREVOR. Could you not?

DANNY. Sorry.

TREVOR. Just do your–

DANNY. OK, OK.

*(Beat. **TREVOR** reads. **DANNY** tries to type, eventually giving up and shutting his laptop.)*

Should I go and–?

TREVOR. Danny, sit still and just, like, shut up, OK?

DANNY. Cool.

*(**DANNY** sits and watches **TREVOR** read. **TREVOR** turns one last page and finishes. He looks at **DANNY**. Beat.)*

Seriously, you're killing me.

TREVOR. It's…

DANNY. Yeah?

TREVOR. I don't know…

DANNY. Oh, Jesus. Just say.

TREVOR. It makes me want to, like, donkey punch you.

DANNY. Yeah?

TREVOR. Yeah.

DANNY. Oh, man. Oh fuck, oh man. I honestly had no idea. I mean, no idea.

TREVOR. Well, get one. It's effin' awesome.

DANNY. Oh my god.

TREVOR. Did you show Pete?

DANNY. Nope.

TREVOR. You didn't show Pete?

DANNY. No, sir. You're first.

TREVOR. Why'm I first?

DANNY. You just are.

TREVOR. Pete's gonna be pissed.

DANNY. He might. Fuck 'im. You're first.

TREVOR. Oooo, he's gonna kill me.

DANNY. He's gonna kill *me*.

TREVOR. Why didn't you show Pete?

DANNY. He's next, don't worry. I needed to show you.

TREVOR. Danny…

DANNY. I was a total girl about it.

TREVOR. Well, show Pete.

DANNY. I will, I will!

(*Beat.*)

So?

TREVOR. Just give me a second. I'm still, you know, processing?

DANNY. Well, could you process with, like, words and shit?

TREVOR. OK. It's not… It's not like anything you've done.

DANNY. I know.

TREVOR. At all.

DANNY. Yeah.

TREVOR. I don't mean just the obvious.

DANNY. No, I know.

TREVOR. It's so lean. It's so... produce-able.

DANNY. Really?

TREVOR *(imitating him)* "Really?" C'mon. That *is* girly.

DANNY. OK.

TREVOR. Four characters? One set? I mean, it could be *done*, you know?

DANNY. I know.

TREVOR. That's almost beside the point though. It's taut. It's mean. It feels very... I hate this word... authentic.

DANNY. As in...?

TREVOR. As in, like, right now. You know?

DANNY. I think it might be good.

TREVOR. I think it might be, too.

DANNY. Oh, man.

(TREVOR *laughs.*)

I mean, god. I was so freakin' nervous. That's why I couldn't show Pete.

TREVOR. Well don't be. Show 'im.

DANNY. I will.

(Beat.)

TREVOR. Danny, this is...

DANNY. Yeah, I know.

TREVOR. How did you...?

DANNY. I have no clue. It just happened. You know that thing where people say, "I didn't write it, it wrote itself"? Those assholes? It's such bullshit.

TREVOR. It's bullshit.

DANNY. Well, I didn't write it. It wrote itself.

TREVOR. You're an asshole.

DANNY. I know!

TREVOR. You have literally no experience to inform it.

DANNY. No shit.

TREVOR. It'll be the first thing people ask.

DANNY. It will?

TREVOR. Um, yeah.

DANNY. So I'll have to come up with a clever answer.

TREVOR. Is there one?

DANNY. I'm a clever little fella.

(Beat.)

Thanks, Trev.

TREVOR. Oh, jeez, no charge, man.

DANNY. No, you don't know.

TREVOR. I might.

DANNY. It's been…

TREVOR. Yeah.

DANNY. You know, the readings, the dirty basements, four years. Four fuckin' years.

TREVOR. I know, I know.

DANNY. If I get one more well-intentioned you-almost-made-it, we-almost-would-maybe-think-about-doing-it-at-some-unforseeable-point-in-the-not-to-be-delineated-future letter, I'll start taking out old ladies in the park.

TREVOR. OK.

DANNY. I'm serious. I thought this would be much easier.

TREVOR. You did?

DANNY. Yeah.

TREVOR. Then you're a dickhead. You've been pretty lucky.

DANNY. Lucky?

TREVOR. Yeah.

DANNY. Three readings in four years? That's not luck, that's a deathwatch.

TREVOR. Jesus, Danny, you just had a reading at–

DANNY. They fuckin'–

TREVOR. So they passed. Boo fuckin' hoo.

DANNY. But a reading is so pathetic. I want people to, I don't know, *see* one of the fuckers, OK?

TREVOR. It's not like you're forty or thirty-five or whatever. It's gonna happen.

DANNY. But I don't wanna turn, you know... I'm gonna be fuckin'–

TREVOR. Dude, you make the path. You make it. Remember?

DANNY. OK.

TREVOR. Just sayin'.

DANNY. Thanks, man.

TREVOR. Whatever.

DANNY. For all the... Ah, shit, you–

TREVOR. Danny. Whatever. OK?

DANNY. OK.

(*Beat.*)

TREVOR. Hey, what's it called?

DANNY. Oh. Yeah.

(*He takes a title page out of his pocket, clips it to the script and sets it back down on the table.* **TREVOR** *looks at it. Beat.*)

TREVOR. Jesus Herbert Walker Christ.

DANNY. Yeah. I know.

TREVOR. That's, that's... Dude, you're gonna hafta be a little more than clever.

DANNY. No shit.

(*Beat.*)

I was thinking of sending it out. If you thought it was OK. You know, resident theatres. Festivals. Dialogue sample. Synopsis. Blind fuckin' hope. The usual.

TREVOR. Well, I thought it was OK.

DANNY. So I should... submit it?

TREVOR. Yup.

DANNY. Submit this bitch?

(*Beat.*)

TREVOR. I think you should submit the fuck out of it.

(*Blackout.*)

Scene 2

(*Danny and Pete's Apartment*)

(**DANNY** *and* **PETE** *sit on the couch, the script on the coffee table in front of them.*)

DANNY. You should be less pissed.

PETE. Oh yeah?

DANNY. Yeah. Less pissed and more... happy. Or something.

PETE. OK, I'm less pissed. I'm more something.

DANNY. OK.

PETE. How long?

DANNY. Petey...

PETE. How long?

DANNY. Two months. But if you'd just–

PETE. You showed him two–

DANNY. Maybe three.

PETE. Three months?

DANNY. Maybe.

PETE. Well, gee, let's start right off with fuck you. You showed him three months ago?

DANNY. Yeah. But I–

PETE. Well, I'm so goddamn relieved it's legal for you kids to get married now. Where ya registered? Sur la Table? Fuckin' Crate and–

DANNY. Babe, just–

PETE. OK. OK.

(*Beat.*)

OK. I'll let that go.

DANNY. Good.

PETE. I said I'll let *that* go.

DANNY. Ugh.

PETE. Because it's really just the tip of the, you know, the fuckin' polar ice cap.

DANNY. Pete, I didn't show you because I thought you'd be... un... uncomfortable?

PETE. I'd be uncomfortable?

DANNY. Yeah.

PETE. Well, the news flash is I wasn't even the littlest bit uncomfortable until you just said you thought I might be uncomfortable. Now? I'm a little uncomfortable.

DANNY. Then I take it back!

PETE. I mean, I wouldn't have been uncomfortable two, three months ago, but being bumped to second on the list of interested readers makes me reconsider my position.

DANNY. Well, technically–

PETE. Technically?

DANNY. I mean, on *my* list, yeah, second.

PETE. What other goddamn list is there?

DANNY. It's a theoretical list.

PETE. What the fuck does that even–

DANNY. Can I just–

PETE. The list of people you may or may not have sent your wonderful new–

DANNY. Wonderful?

PETE. No, no, you shut up. This list is somehow theoretical?

DANNY. You think it's wonderful.

PETE. I think it's less wonderful the more you open your yap, so be careful.

DANNY. Petey, I... submitted it places.

PETE. Ah.

DANNY. And now–

PETE. No, no. Let me just… So, you write this–

DANNY. Wonder–

PETE. Danny.

DANNY. Sorry.

PETE. You write this thing, you show it to your boyfriend Trevor, you submit it to god knows where–

DANNY. Several places. Good places.

PETE. Whatever. And then, then, at the end of all this, you stoop, you deign to show it to me. I'm… I'm touched, baby. I'm really touched.

DANNY. Look.

PETE. No, you look.

DANNY. Look, babe, just let me–

PETE. It's humiliating, you know?

DANNY. How is it humiliating? You're the only person in the wide stupid galaxy that knows I didn't show you first. I didn't–

PETE. Everybody–

DANNY. Oh my god, you shut up now. You. Shut up. OK? Shut up.

PETE. But you–

DANNY. Shut up! I didn't show you first because I was scared. OK?

PETE. That's the most–

DANNY. I was scared. Not of your reaction to the obvious shit. That's not it. I was scared it wasn't good.

PETE. Oh, baby–

DANNY. Or not good enough. That you wouldn't think I was good. Or that you might think I was… I dunno. You know. And that *was* because of the obvious shit. And then I showed Trev, because I had to show it to somebody, and he said it was good, and then I couldn't show you because I decided to start sending it around and I didn't want to have this very conversation and then a week went by and another week and then a month, and I just let it go.

PETE. You let it–

DANNY. And by then I hadn't shown it to you so I couldn't show it to you, and that's where I made my mistake.

PETE. *That's* where?

DANNY. OK, that's one of the places–

PETE. Many places–

DANNY. Many places I made a mistake. OK? But now I had to show. And you already said it's–

PETE. Wait.

DANNY. What?

PETE. Why?

DANNY. Why what?

PETE. Why now?

(Beat.)

Danny, why now?

DANNY. Because it got…

PETE. Danny?

DANNY. It got accepted.

PETE. What?

DANNY. It got accepted.

PETE. Baby…

DANNY. They called today, it got accepted. So maybe stop being pissed and, like, kiss me or something.

PETE. For a reading?

DANNY. No. No. No. Not for a goddamn reading. It got accepted for a goddamn production at the goddamn Humana Festival–

PETE. Is that a big deal?

DANNY. Are you fucking– Petey, they're going to produce my goddamn, goddamn, goddamn play, so could you stop being pissed for just long enough to jump up and down a little with me? Please?

*(Beat. **PETE** and **DANNY** jump up and down.)*

PETE. Oh Jesus, oh Jesus, oh god!

DANNY. I know! I know!

PETE. Danny, that's...

DANNY. I know!

PETE. I'm sorry, I'm sorry, I was thinking about–

DANNY. No, you're right, I should've shown you right away.
But they're going to do it, babe, they're going to do
it. With people in it, with people watching it, with sets
and costumes and ticket takers and ushers and fuck-
tard critics and shit.

PETE. Oh my god.

DANNY. I know!

*(**PETE** kisses **DANNY**. They settle onto the couch. Beat.
PETE picks up the script for a moment and looks at the
title page.)*

PETE. You're gonna get shit about this.

DANNY. Um...

PETE. You know?

DANNY. Yeah, that's not actually the title page.

PETE. That's not the title?

DANNY. Well, that's the title, but that's not the title page I
submitted to Humana.

PETE. Whaddya mean?

*(**DANNY** pulls out a new title page from his pocket and
smoothes it onto the script. Beat.)*

You're a fuckin' idiot.

DANNY. Yeah.

PETE. You are.

DANNY. I know.

PETE. What are you going to do?

DANNY. I don't have a fuckin' clue.

(Blackout.)

Scene 3

(Another Coffee Chain)

*(December. Coats, hats. **DANNY** and **EMILIE** sit at a small table that only has room for one cup of coffee and the script, which lies between them.)*

EMILIE. I don't understand.

DANNY. Well, let me–

EMILIE. You're the director?

DANNY. No.

EMILIE. You're not the director?

DANNY. No. Who told you I was the director?

EMILIE. You did, didn't you?

DANNY. No.

EMILIE. You didn't?

DANNY. No.

EMILIE. I really don't under–

DANNY. I'm sorry. Let's start again.

EMILIE. That's OK. I misunderstood.

DANNY. Probably not.

EMILIE. I'm not right for this anyway.

DANNY. You're perfect. Look, I saw you in that Donatella Frazetti thing at New Georges last year, I think you're great.

EMILIE. Thank you.

DANNY. You're perfect for this.

EMILIE. I'm not. The mother is maybe twenty years older than me. I couldn't play it. It would be weird.

DANNY. It's not for the play.

EMILIE. Obviously.

DANNY. It's for the playwright.

   (Beat.)

EMILIE. Excuse me?

DANNY. It's for the playwright. I told your agent it was for the play because I didn't know how else to get you to meet with me. It's a little bit of a misrepresentation–

EMILIE. A little bit?

DANNY. I'm sorry.

EMILIE. I should go. This is too weird.

(She gets up to go.)

DANNY. Wait. Emilie, please. Please.

(Beat.)

Let me explain. Just let me explain and then you can go. But it's nothing weird, or at least not the kind of weird you should leave because of. I'm gay. I'm very gay. So, there's nothing weird here.

EMILIE. Very gay?

DANNY. Well, yeah.

(She inches back to the table; she doesn't sit back down.)

EMILIE. So you're not the director.

DANNY. No.

EMILIE. And I'm not right for the part.

DANNY. No.

EMILIE. All right, you've got two minutes. But then I'm going.

DANNY. Fair enough.

EMILIE. So…

DANNY. Sorry. So I wrote this play.

EMILIE. You're the playwright?

DANNY. Yeah.

EMILIE. So who's this?

(She points to the title page.)

DANNY. Hopefully you.

EMILIE. OK, you're not making any–

DANNY. I wrote the play. But I think it's pretty clear why I'd be a little… um… unsure about people's response to

me being the author. And so when I sent it out
world, out for people to look at, I put anothe
on it. I put this name on it. Because I thought, a
is where I'm pretty sure I'm looking like a big big tool,
that if it wasn't some name like "Danny Larson" on this
play, this particular play, people might actually read
it. Might think about reading it. So I put this name
on it. And I never expected, I mean hoped, certainly,
but never expected anybody to pick up the thing,
because it's my fifth full-length and nobody's jumped
at anything yet, so I had no idea how that would feel,
how that would go. And when the phone call came, I
panicked and said I was the playwright's cousin and
I'd give her the message and that was a week ago and
I haven't... had the balls to call them back and tell
them the truth, and they've been emailing me... well,
emailing her to start scheduling meetings with directors and things and I think that if I show up, if this
who-the-fuck-is-he white guy shows up they'll pull the
plug on the whole thing and I think that might leave
me completely unable to write another word. Forever.
So I looked through old Playbills, because I save them
all, because I think I mentioned I'm very gay...

EMILIE. Uh-huh...

DANNY. And remembered you and found your agent,
because your union may be the Island of Misfit Toys,
but handing out phone numbers they apparently
can do, and got to you. And here you are. And I was
hoping you would let me try to talk you into a little
acting job. For pay. And that's the whole thing and you
can go now if you want.

(*Beat.*)

EMILIE. That's–

DANNY. I know.

EMILIE. That's whacked out, that's... But it seems to me
you should just tell them you wrote the thing. Whoever
"them" is.

DANNY. It's the Humana Festival.

EMILIE. What?

DANNY. Humana.

EMILIE. Oh my god.

DANNY. It could truly make me. And if I tell them I pulled the wool over their eyes and they take a dump on me, it would probably break me.

(She sits back down.)

EMILIE. But they're going to find out.

DANNY. I know.

EMILIE. I mean, they'd have to.

DANNY. I want them to. But not before they've produced the thing.

EMILIE. That's not–

DANNY. I know. I know. It's cocoa puffs, I know, I know it, but I honestly think they'll scuttle the whole thing if I tell them now. But if the show is a success and then I tell them… Or *we* tell them…

EMILIE. And they–

DANNY. It's not about publicity, although I'm sure it would generate that. It's about legitimizing the play.

EMILIE. Huh.

DANNY. Which I think, I know it's good. It's–

EMILIE. It's very good.

DANNY. And I don't want to screw this up.

EMILIE. Any more than you have.

DANNY. Um… yeah.

EMILIE. So what would I do?

DANNY. Well, you'd be her.

(He points to the script.)

EMILIE. OK. If I do this–

DANNY. Oh, Jesus, that's–

EMILIE. *If* I do this.

DANNY. OK.

EMILIE. I'm not her. I mean, I'm no star, but I do have a career, or am starting to have one. I haven't worked at Humana, but I've auditioned for them and last year I was called back twice for one of the plays, so they know who I am.

DANNY. All the better.

EMILIE. How do you figure?

DANNY. Easy for you to say you put another name on it because as an actress you didn't want to get dismissed as another actress-turned-writer.

EMILIE. As opposed to...?

DANNY. A white dude writing a play about an alcoholic black mother and her card-sharp son trying to get out of the Projects.

EMILIE. And the title of his play is... *Call A Spade.*

DANNY. And the title of his play is *Call A Spade.* And he is very much afraid his play would be immediately dismissed because he is a white, white dude.

EMILIE. So you wanna pull some *Freaky Friday* shit with me.

DANNY. More like some *Victor/Victoria* shit, I think.

EMILIE. Huh. You are very gay.

DANNY. Yes, ma'am.

EMILIE. God.

DANNY. I know.

EMILIE. Well, first of all...

DANNY. Yeah?

(She points to the script.)

EMILIE. This isn't even a real name.

DANNY. It's not supposed to be your real name.

EMILIE. I mean, it's not a name. I don't even know how you'd say it. Shaleeha Nahgoa... What?

DANNY. Shaleeha G'ntamobi. *(sha-LEE-ya guh-NAH-ta-MOH-bee)*

EMILIE. Shaleeha G'ntamobi.

DANNY. Yeah.

EMILIE. You said it so easily.

DANNY. I've been practicing.

EMILIE. That's not a name. It's just a bunch of sounds put together. Where'd you get it?

DANNY. I just tried to think of a name that sounded kind of…

(Beat.)

EMILIE. Black.

DANNY. Yeah. Is that bad?

EMILIE. It ain't good.

DANNY. Yeah… Well…

EMILIE. And what happens to me?

DANNY. When?

EMILIE. When you are revealed to be the white dude who pretended to be Shaleeha Nohgoh–

DANNY. G'Ntamobi.

EMILIE. Whatever. What happens to me?

DANNY. Well, I haven't figured that out. But on top of whatever you get in a salary-type way for the next couple months, you get points in the show. When it gets produced. Hopefully all over the fuckin' world.

EMILIE. I get points?

DANNY. Sure.

EMILIE. In writing?

DANNY. Of course. I mean, we're not animals.

EMILIE. And then what?

DANNY. And we both quit our day jobs, not to assume you've got a day job…

EMILIE. Assume away.

DANNY. And get royalty checks for the rest of our days. Or at least some of our days.

EMILIE. Does that really happen?

DANNY. It better.

(Beat.)

EMILIE. It's just... It's good. People should see it.

DANNY. So...

EMILIE. But this is fucked up.

DANNY. A little bit.

EMILIE. And...

DANNY. And...?

EMILIE. Are we talking googobs of money?

DANNY. Oh, Emilie. I certainly fuckin' hope so.

   (Blackout.)

Scene 4

(Danny and Pete's Apartment)

(EMILIE is on the phone, holding the script. DANNY is sitting close by, intent on her. PETE and TREVOR are watching the whole thing, in horror or amusement or some strange combination.)

EMILIE. No. No. It's pronounced G'Ntamobi... Yeah, I guess pronunciation isn't so important if it's not real.

DANNY. Careful.

PETE. *(to DANNY)* Shut up, babe.

EMILIE. Huh. That's a good... Uh... I was scared, I guess. I mean, I thought it was OK, but I figured anybody who knew me would think I was just another dumb actress who decided writing a play must be easy.

TREVOR. You mean it isn't?

DANNY. Fuck off.

EMILIE. Yeah, well... I can't believe it was selected.

DANNY. Excuse me?

PETE. Babe, just–

EMILIE. I'm such a fan, you know? All of my favorite American plays in the last ten years have started with you guys, it seems.

DANNY. Well, Jesus, don't go crazy.

   (EMILIE gestures to DANNY to get away.)

PETE. Danny, heel.

DANNY. But—

EMILIE. Thanks. I can't wait to meet him. And I'll see you next month. Anything else you need from me, you can call me on my cell.

DANNY. Or here.

EMILIE. *(to* **PETE***)* Could you...?

(**PETE** *puts his hand over* **DANNY**'*s mouth.* **EMILIE** *goes back to the phone.)*

EMILIE. Or this number, I guess, but my cell is where you can reach me— Oh, that's... that's— Thanks so much, Mister Thomp— OK. Barry.

DANNY. *(muffled)* Barry?

EMILIE. Talk to you soon. Bye.

(She hangs up. **PETE** *lets* **DANNY** *go. They all stare at her. Beat..)*

DANNY. Well?

EMILIE. You're not going to believe it.

DANNY. What?

EMILIE. This is nuts.

DANNY. What already?

EMILIE. All right. You want a director?

DANNY. Yes, please.

EMILIE. How about Lawrence James?

DANNY. No way.

PETE. Who?

TREVOR. Oh shit.

PETE. Who is—?

DANNY. Oh shit. Oh shit.

EMILIE. Yeah.

PETE. Who the hell is—?

DANNY. Lawrence James directed that thing about Booker T. Washington at The Public last year.

TREVOR. Went to Broadway.

EMILIE. Yup.

TREVOR. He won a–

DANNY. It was on PBS last month.

PETE. Oh. Well, I love PBS.

DANNY. Holy shit! Holy holy shit!

EMILIE. He was very understanding about–

DANNY. Lawrence Ja–?

EMILIE. No. Sorry. Barry Thompson was understanding about–

PETE. Oh, c'mon, who is Barry–?

DANNY. From Humana.

TREVOR. Literary guy.

DANNY. He's in charge of–

TREVOR. Choosing.

DANNY. Choosing. Judging. Crippling writers with doubt and worry.

TREVOR. British accent. Born in Topeka.

PETE. All right, all right.

EMILIE Said he totally understood about the actress thing. And since they're about to announce they just need to figure out the best way to put out my name. They may wait until it's closer.

DANNY. Wow.

EMILIE. They just don't want any inkling of impropriety, he said.

TREVOR. Inkling?

EMILIE. Inkling.

TREVOR. He said inkling?

EMILIE. He said inkling.

TREVOR. Say it again.

EMILIE. Inkling.

TREVOR. Inkling.

EMILIE. Inkling.

TREVOR. Ink–

DANNY. Um, hello?

EMILIE. Sorry.

TREVOR. Sorry.

(*Beat.*)

Inkling.

(**EMILIE** *and* **TREVOR** *laugh*)

DANNY. C'mon.

EMILIE. (*To* **TREVOR**) You're funny.

TREVOR. Well, shucks.

DANNY. Oh my god. Can we–?

EMILIE. Sorry.

TREVOR. Sorry.

DANNY. So what–

EMILIE. Nothing. Nothing for now. They'll call in a couple weeks to set up auditions, press will start calling then too, they're announcing the line-up next week, so he said I should get ready.

PETE. Get ready?

EMILIE. "Get ready to get famous."

(*Beat.*)

Is what he said.

DANNY. Get ready to get famous?

EMILIE. Yeah.

TREVOR. Oh my god, it's a freakin' disaster movie.

DANNY. It's all gonna be fine. It's all gonna–

EMILIE. Yeah.

PETE. Uh-huh.

(*Beat.*)

EMILIE. I'm so fucking excited about this!

DANNY. Right?

PETE. This is good, isn't it?

DANNY. It's very–

TREVOR. It's good.

PETE. Well, it's about time. I'm all for early retirement.

DANNY. Fuck, yeah.

PETE. You're cute when you're successful.

DANNY. That's right I am.

EMILIE. *(to* **DANNY***)* He's funny, too. *(to* **PETE***)* You're all quiet and Brooks Brothers and then look out. I like it.

PETE. *(imitating* **TREVOR***)* Well, shucks.

(**TREVOR** *laughs.*)

EMILIE. You sure you're not an actor?

PETE. God, no.

EMILIE. What do you–

PETE. I make money for people who already have money.

EMILIE. Oh, you're a monster.

PETE. Nah. Just a realist.

EMILIE. Wow. You guys are, like, hardly gay at all.

(*Beat.*)

PETE. You'd be surprised.

EMILIE. *(re:* **DANNY** *and* **TREVOR***)* And you two met–?

TREVOR. Grad school.

EMILIE. Gotcha. Which was where?

TREVOR. In New Haven.

DANNY. Jesus. He can't even say the word.

TREVOR. It's so braggy.

DANNY. See?

EMILIE. *(to* **TREVOR***)* You know, I've met you before.

TREVOR. You have?   **DANNY.** You know him?

EMILIE. I was your reader for that thing at the–

TREVOR. Oh, shit. I thought you looked–

EMILIE. You know? For that–

TREVOR. That was so epically stupid.

EMILIE. I thought you got it.

TREVOR. So did I.

EMILIE. Fuckers.

TREVOR. Yeah. Fuckers.

EMILIE. Yeah.

> (**EMILIE** *stares at* **TREVOR.** *Beat. Then, still looking at* **TREVOR.**)

I... gotta go.

DANNY. You do?

EMILIE. Yeah. *(to* **TREVOR***)* You wanna split a cab?

TREVOR. I do.

PETE. *(grabbing* **DANNY***)* Cabs! Baby, our early retirement is gonna be full of cabs.

EMILIE. *(to* **DANNY***)* So, Friday?

DANNY. Yeah, Friday.

TREVOR. What's Friday?

DANNY. We gotta start figuring out–

PETE. 'enry 'iggins here has to get Eliza Doolittle all ready for the ball. The ball! Oh my god. The ball! *(He sings a bit.)* "I could've danced all night. I could've–" *(to* **DANNY***)* Baby! We're in a fuckin' musical!

EMILIE. *(to* **DANNY***)* I take it back. He's very gay, too.

DANNY. God I hope so.

> (**DANNY** *and* **PETE** *kiss.*)

EMILIE. Oh my god, get a fuckin' room.

PETE. Look around. We did.

DANNY. So, see you–

EMILIE. Yeah.

PETE. You got your...?

EMILIE. Got it. Thanks for... you know... including me in your strange little crime.

DANNY. It's not a–

EMILIE. Kidding, Danny, kidding. *(to* **TREVOR***)* You comin'?

TREVOR. Hey, I'm walking, too– Hold on.

EMILIE. All right, c'mon.

TREVOR. I'm comin', I'm comin. Bah.

DANNY. Bah.

EMILIE. Night.

PETE. Bye.

> (**TREVOR, DANNY,** *and* **PETE** *exchange hugs, whatever.*
> **EMILIE** *and* **TREVOR** *exit. Beat.*)
>
> Is it a—?

DANNY. It's not a crime!

PETE. Danny…

DANNY. Crime is a big word. Crime is robbing a child. Strangling your mom and gutting her puppy. Invading a country without cause. This is not a crime.

PETE. Then why'd she—?

DANNY. It's not a fuckin' crime!

> (**DANNY** *takes* **PETE** *in his arms*)
>
> It's just a fuckin' play.
>
> (*Blackout.*)

Scene 5

> (*Another Coffee Chain*)
>
> (*January. Still coats, hats.* **DANNY** *and* **EMILIE** *sit at a medium-sized table, coffee and pages from the script all over the table between them.*)

DANNY. I think you just say "I don't know."

EMILIE. Oh, c'mon.

DANNY. I do.

EMILIE. I can't.

DANNY. I think you say something along the lines of "I don't know" or "hopefully the play answers that question" or something like that.

EMILIE. But that's so pretentious.

DANNY. Exactly.

EMILIE. I'm not kidding.

DANNY. I'm not either. You're the writer. You just refer them back to the play and get all humbly and tongue-tied and they'll think you're smart.

EMILIE. So I'm supposed to sit in some production meeting–

DANNY. Yes.

EMILIE. or some one-on-one with the director–

DANNY. Yeah. Yes.

EMILIE. and say, "Gosh, I hope the play answers that question" and that'll shut them up?

DANNY. If you try to explain the thing to 'em, they'll start to hold you up to your explanation, and I gotta tell you, Em, if they do that you're absolutely fucked.

EMILIE. And when I bring the questions back to you?

DANNY. I'll say I think the play answers the question.

EMILIE. That is such tremendous horseshit!

DANNY. I know! Isn't it awesome?

EMILIE. You should never've told me the secret, you know?

DANNY. I'll just have to trust you.

EMILIE. Guess so.

DANNY. Yup.

(They both laugh. Beat. She shuffles through the pages in front of them.)

EMILIE. Danny?

DANNY. Hmm?

EMILIE. Really, where'd this come from?

DANNY. I don't–

EMILIE. Yeah, yeah. I'm in the club now, Danny.

DANNY. Well, shit. You really wanna–?

EMILIE. Yes!

DANNY. All right, all right. So, I'm sitting on the subway with Pete last year just, you know, going home.

EMILIE. Your subway?

DANNY. Which subway would it be?

EMILIE. Sorry.

DANNY. And there's these kids, maybe twelve, ___ talking real loud, real instrusive-like, and everybody's trying hard not to notice them.

EMILIE. Black kids?

DANNY. Well, yeah.

EMILIE. OK.

DANNY. Why?

EMILIE. Just getting the picture.

DANNY. OK. And one of them, I see, is pointing to my shoes, and my shoes are, I think, kinda cool. And kinda like the shoes one of them is wearing, I guess. So I think they're noticing that I'm kinda cool. Which makes me look up and maybe more actively notice them, you know?

EMILIE. Sure.

DANNY. And then I hear the one kid say something about "shoes a homo would wear" and I'm, like, stunned. I can't believe it. And I look at Pete and he's trying real hard–

EMILIE. Not to notice.

DANNY. Not to notice, yeah. And I'm fascinated by them, but now I'm pissed, too. And I want to take more of this in, because that thing in my head, that there's-an-idea-over-there-try-not-to-scare-it-away thing that happens when I want to write starts making loud alarm-type sounds, but I can't stop myself and I get all, "Hey, kid, that is so not cool."

EMILIE. You go, girl.

DANNY. And he gets a little up in my face, not a lot, but enough, and I try to stand my ground, and Pete keeps trying not to notice and eventually they move further down the car.

EMILIE. Uh-huh.

DANNY. And now this kid is in my head, his voice, what he said, how he looked, his friends, what they said, the feel of it all, the way it... I dunno, grabbed me, and for the next week I can't get away from it, and I think it's because I got my feelings a little banged up, because I don't wanna be the homo with the shoes, but the truth is, I want to know about that kid, and that's fuckin' death for me. Because once I want to know about somebody, then I gotta sit down and stare at my angry little computer and I'm totally, completely and utterly fucked. Because I sit down and the cursor goes blink, blink and it's this kid that I know absolutely nothing about who wants to talk, and, Emilie, I won't lie to you, it was completely terrifying, but I couldn't stop. Because he had stuff to say, and then his mom, and his brother and that little girl from down the block, and then, when everybody's done talking, I've got this play. That nobody is going to look at. Ever. And, Jesus Christ, what now?

EMILIE. Huh.

DANNY. Yeah.

(*Beat.*)

You know, you can say what you think about it.

EMILIE. What?

DANNY. About the play, I can take it.

EMILIE. I did say. I like it.

DANNY. I'm a big boy.

EMILIE. Danny, I like it.

DANNY. Really, I'm tough.

EMILIE. I love it.

DANNY. Oh thank god.

EMILIE. I really do. It's beyond me how you did it, but it's so, so good.

DANNY. It's actually beyond me too.

EMILIE. And it pisses me off a little, I think.

DANNY. Yeah?

EMILIE. Because you got it so right.

DANNY. Oh.

EMILIE. That's all.

DANNY. Oh.

EMILIE. And you should be, whatever... I think you should maybe be a little more...

DANNY. Look, however not freaked out about this you think I am, I'm about, I don't know, four hundred and sisty-seven times more freaked out than you think.

EMILIE. Yeah?

DANNY. Hand to god.

EMILIE. Good.

(*Beat. They both thumb through the play.*)

EMILIE. I wasn't kidding, you know.

DANNY. What?

EMILIE. I love it.

DANNY. Aw...

EMILIE. It's... There's so much... This little girl stuff here, she's so–

DANNY. Thanks.

EMILIE. The thing with the dog. God, that scene where the–

DANNY. Which–

EMILIE. The mom takes the knife away from him, but puts it in a drawer–

DANNY. Oh, yeah.

EMILIE. Just within reach because it's "important to know what you're capable of."

DANNY. You don't think that's a little–

EMILIE. Oh, god no.

DANNY. Well, thanks.

EMILIE. It's important to... where'd you...?

DANNY. I told you. I. Don't. Know.

EMILIE. C'mon.

DANNY. No! That's why it's so good to use, because, like, seven times out of twelve, it's just fuckin' true. That's a tip I'm passin' along in case you ever write somethin' of your own.

EMILIE. Me? Please.

DANNY. It could happen.

EMILIE. I'm full up on rejection, but thanks. Although... Oh, fuck it.

DANNY. What?

EMILIE. No, no. Fuck it.

DANNY. Emilie, what?

EMILIE. OK. Are we... I dunno.

DANNY. Honestly no idea what's going on right now.

EMILIE. I just... I thought it would be...

DANNY. Oh my god, are you having, like, a stroke or something?

EMILIE. What if the little girl walked in right then?

(Beat.)

DANNY. Oh.

EMILIE. Forget it.

DANNY. No, no...

EMILIE. I don't–

DANNY. I just–

EMILIE. Look. I'm either sitting here like some weird, whatever, some fuckin' puppet, or–

DANNY. You're not a–

EMILIE. Or I'm part of this. You know?

DANNY. Yeah...

EMILIE. And I'd rather be part of it.

DANNY. OK.

EMILIE. And I don't know thing number one about puttin' pen to paper, or what goes on in you or anybody when that happens but–

DANNY. It's OK. I... Here's the thing, right? This... this... It happens alone. I mean that's my... I dunno... That's my experience of it...

EMILIE. Sorry, I didn't–

DANNY. No, no, no, I... It's gotta come from me, is all. Like it's my only chance, now, before anybody says it out loud, it's the only time it's all mine. And I... I... I like that.

EMILIE. OK, so I should–

DANNY. I really like it. But that time might be gone now, is my point. It might be gone. So...

EMILIE. What?

DANNY. So maybe the little girl walks in right then.

EMILIE. Oh.

DANNY. Maybe.

EMILIE. Maybe.

DANNY. Maybe.

(Beat.)

EMILIE. Danny?

DANNY. Yeah?

EMILIE. This is fuckin' great.

DANNY. Yeah.

EMILIE. Oh my god. This is–

DANNY. Welcome to the club.

EMILIE. What happens when it's all over?

DANNY. Whaddya mean?

EMILIE. After the festival?

DANNY. We get famous, right? You're so awesome being... well... me, that somebody notices you and whisks you away and you win a Blony for some stupid revival and I get a–

EMILIE. What?

DANNY. You know, a remount of some forgotten 30's social–

EMILIE. Wait, wait. My what?

DANNY. Your what what?

EMILIE. I win my what?

DANNY. Your Blony! You know, the Tony somebody wins, usually some supporting actor or actress or whatever, the award they win that seems a little suspect, like they won it maybe because everybody else was all–

EMILIE. A black Tony?

DANNY. Yeah! There are Blonys, Bloscars, you know... Some reality show reject sings a sad, sad song and it's "the envelope please!"

EMILIE. Danny, that's–

DANNY. Or if somebody is all "whatchoo talkin' about" in some play or movie, they're doin' some real Blacting, you know? Or my play, you know, I need four Blactors to be in it.

(Beat.)

What? Did I say somethin' wrong?

EMILIE. Um...

DANNY. What?

EMILIE. Do you think you didn't?

DANNY. C'mon, you've heard that before.

EMILIE. Not from...

DANNY. Yeah, yeah, I know, but it's funny, right?

EMILIE. It's pretty much not funny at all.

DANNY. Oh, jeez, c'mon. C'mon Emilie, funny's funny. No harm, no... you know.

EMILIE. Um, OK, but reducing, I dunno, let's say... you talking last year?

DANNY. OK, sure, last year.

EMILIE. Reducing that life-changing award that woman won last year for her beautiful, terrific work–

DANNY. It was a seven-minute–

EMILIE. Wait a–

DANNY. A seven-minute scene in a two-and-a-half hour play, Emilie.

EMILIE. So?

DANNY. So a seven-minute scene with a big freaky monologue about a circus clown and all sorts of portents of mumbo-jumbo doom and speechifying and poof: Tony!

EMILIE. That's fuckin' right.

DANNY. It's a Blony!

EMILIE. You saying she didn't deserve it? She was amazing.

DANNY. Well, I dunno. I guess she did. She was good, sure.

EMILIE. But it was a Blony?

DANNY. Well, she's black, she won a Tony, it was... a... Blony.

(Beat.)

OK. But you've never said it? Heard it? I don't believe that for a second.

EMILIE. I've heard it, sure, but there's a... whatever you... there's a code, you know?

DANNY. Oh, Jesus.

EMILIE. There is!

DANNY. You can say it but I can't.

EMILIE. Fuckin' right.

DANNY. See, that's bullshit.

EMILIE. OK. So, like, every time a gay guy wins a choreography award over some straight choreographer–

DANNY. What's a straight choreographer?

EMILIE. or some really deserving, amazing, female choreographer, it's not at all because he's in the gay mafia or anything.

DANNY. Here we go.

EMILIE. You started it.

DANNY. OK. Maybe. But that's such an old-timey way of thinking about things.

EMILIE. Are you serious now?

DANNY. And besides, it's not the same thing at all.

EMILIE. What I just said is not the same as what you just said.

DANNY. No.

EMILIE. At all.

DANNY. No. No.

EMILIE. You are so full of shit your eyes are brown! I don't even know what to–

DANNY. Look, Emilie, I know what it's like.

EMILIE. You what?

DANNY. I know what it's like to be all, you know, all ghetto-ized, I know it. I've been there. I've felt it every day of my life since I figured out I was gay.

EMILIE. OK. Wait. We should stop. You're about to get yourself in some bad, bad trouble, and I think we should stop.

DANNY. No, no, listen, I'm just saying I know what it's like. Prejudice, you know? The big world and all that, turning against you, against me. I've been there. I'm there. We're the same.

EMILIE. Danny, if you're going to sit there and tell me that my life as a black woman in this society, in this particular society, the United States of Whatever, is somehow, in some way, in *any* way, comparable to your middle-class realization that you like dick more than not, then you are living in a ridiculously large world of crazy and I'm kind of, I can't even think of a big enough word, flabbergasted. Seriously.

DANNY. OK. We're not the same. That was the wrong thing to say.

EMILIE. You think?

DANNY. But I'm saying I know some of what you know.

EMILIE. Kid, you don't know a single thing I know.

DANNY. Now, c'mon.

EMILIE. No, you can't.

DANNY. Now who's being stubborn?

EMILIE. Stubborn?

DANNY. You're gonna tell me that when I was eighteen and some guy followed me out of a bar near my dorm and told me to not come back, because they "don't serve no fags no drinks not ever" that I didn't get some itty bitty window into what it's like to have people hate you just 'cuz of who you are?

EMILIE. No. Because it's not who you are.

DANNY. Excuse me?

EMILIE. Who you sleep with isn't who you are.

DANNY. Well, of course it isn't. Christ.

EMILIE. Who you sleep with is who you sleep with.

DANNY. And being gay isn't who you sleep with. It's who you are.

EMILIE. Oh, man.

DANNY. What?

EMILIE. Take away what happens in your bedroom, and what are you, Danny? Just another white guy walking around telling the world what to do.

DANNY. That's crazy!

EMILIE. And knowing good and goddamn well that the world is probably gonna do it, because you're just another white guy walking around saying it.

DANNY. Well, now I'm getting a little pissed.

EMILIE. Oh, no. Oh, that's terrible. Poor, poor white guy is getting pissed because two minutes of his life stopped going his way. Jesus.

DANNY. I'm not all those guys, Emilie.

EMILIE. No, but you're one of 'em.

DANNY. C'mon.

EMILIE. No, you c'mon. You're a really nice guy, Danny, I know, and I'm gonna give you points for trying, and I'll even give you points for people being mean to you, because I know that gay can't always be easy, I get that, but a gay white guy telling a black woman he gets her pain is a little like Adolf Hitler eating a piece of fuckin' kugel and saying he understands the plight of the Jews. So back off, OK? And quit while you're just a little bit behind, because now I actually am starting to get mad, and that's not good for either one of us. And it's certainly not good for this play. And I know you care more about that than us, so let's stop for the sake of the baby.

(Beat.)

DANNY. OK.

(Beat.)

But can I ask you one thing?

EMILIE. Danny…

DANNY. One thing.

(Beat.)

EMILIE. All right. Shoot.

DANNY. Earlier, when I was telling you about that shoe thing on the subway, right?

EMILIE. Yeah…

DANNY. Not even one second into the story you wanted clarification.

EMILIE. What?

DANNY. I told you there were some boys and you wanted to know if they were black. You wanted to know. I just said they were boys and you wanted to know what we looked like on that train, me and those boys, from a pigment-oriented standpoint.

EMILIE. So?

DANNY. So, I'm not the one who spelled that out, you were. You needed to know. So. Before you get all crazier-than-thou, don't accuse me of not noticing the way the world works. Racially, I mean. Because you made the same assumptions anybody would about that story, and that is because we're all the same. Not because we want to be. But because we are. And the thing that freaks you out, the reason you're even here, because I

know it's going to freak more than just you ⟨
some guy might be able to sit in his middle-⟨
ment and imagine a life that isn't his, a lif
think you have some ownership of, and the thing that
freaks *me* out is that I think, I'm starting to think we all
have ownership of it, and I don't quite know what to
do with that. But I'm not wrong about it. I'm not completely wrong about it. At least not yet.

(Beat.)

OK?

EMILIE. I don't know.

DANNY. OK?

EMILIE. Danny...

DANNY. OK?

(Beat.)

EMILIE. OK.

DANNY. OK.

(Beat.)

EMILIE. For now.

(Blackout.)

Scene 6

(A Hallway)

*(**DANNY** and **TREVOR** sit in two chairs [or on a bench] against a blank wall, looking offstage to an unseen door. **DANNY** is texting on his cell phone. The script is on his lap.)*

DANNY. Shit. This fucking–

TREVOR. Stop doing it so fast, that–

DANNY. Shut up. Shit. Shit.

TREVOR. Dude, you're doing it too–

DANNY. Shut up.

(**TREVOR** *looks around while* **DANNY** *finishes up and sends his text.*)

DANNY. *(cont.)* Sorry.

TREVOR. Whatever, ya dick.

DANNY. Fuckin' smart text totally blows.

TREVOR. It's because you do it too fast.

DANNY. It fucking blows.

TREVOR. OK... And what do they think when Emilie's getting all these texts?

DANNY. They can think whatever they want. It's not like she's responding to all of 'em.

TREVOR. True, but this is all a little douchey, don't you think?

DANNY. It's a best-solution situation.

TREVOR. It's mayonnaise and relish on a poop sandwich. The sandwich is still primarily shit, you know?

DANNY. Hilarious. I just– Oh, hold on.

(**DANNY** *looks off.*)

There goes another one.

(**TREVOR** *looks off.*)

Huh.

TREVOR. What?

DANNY. I gotta look at him when he comes out. He's, like...

TREVOR. What?

DANNY. You know, a little fat I think, a little three-cheese-burgers-away-from-a-medical-intervention, so...

TREVOR. Can I say something a little controversial?

DANNY. Sure.

TREVOR. I'm all in favor of you getting your play done, right?

DANNY. Right.

TREVOR. And this Emilie thing is... I dunno... it is what it is, I guess.

DANNY. OK...

TREVOR. But sitting out here sending texts about your physical impression of poor little actor-bots who are just trying to get a job without even seeing them audition makes me think this whole thing is maybe not gonna go so well.

DANNY. Right. And what about Emilie?

TREVOR. Whaddya mean?

DANNY. What does she think–

TREVOR. How would I know?

DANNY. I dunno. How would you know?

TREVOR. I wouldn't.

DANNY. Really?

TREVOR. Really. What are you–

DANNY. OK, OK.

TREVOR. Look, I don't wanna harsh on you.

DANNY. Do you have a better idea? Like, I mean, I just mean if you have some super fantastic suggestion that might let me be part of the auditions for my skit without having to go in there and announce my honky cracker existence, I'm completely, really, completely open to it. The floor is, like, procedurally, parliamentarily open to the membership giving ideas. So, you got any?

(Beat.)

TREVOR. You don't have to be a total dick about it.

DANNY. I wasn't.

TREVOR. I think I just get to say every once in a while when I, like, disagree, don't I?

DANNY. Of course.

TREVOR. So don't be a total dick when I tell you I'm not in 100 percent agreement with something that I think seems more than a little on the not-healthy side, OK?

DANNY. I'm sorry.

TREVOR. OK?

DANNY. I'm sorry, Trev.

TREVOR. Whatever.

DANNY. Trevor?

TREVOR. What?

DANNY. I'm sorry.

TREVOR. OK.

DANNY. I didn't mean to be a fuckwad.

TREVOR. You just couldn't help it, I guess.

DANNY. I couldn't.

(*Beat.*)

I'm really glad you're here.

TREVOR. I know.

DANNY. Pete gets so, you know, so bummed he can't get time off to come with me when I'm–

TREVOR. Doing stupid, stupid things?

DANNY. Exactly.

TREVOR. Because this is…

DANNY. I know.

TREVOR. Like trying to… stuff a… doberman pincher into a… freakin'… Scooby Doo lunchbox. Or somethin'.

(*Beat. They both laugh.*)

DANNY. Wow.

TREVOR. Yeah, yeah.

DANNY. Just… wow.

TREVOR. Look, joking aside, I just… Fuck… I mean, Pete's not here, you know? I don't wanna get all weird about this, but… Fuck, now I feel stupid.

DANNY. Trev–

TREVOR. No, I mean, you know, I'm the one is what I… I'm the one sitting in this effin' hallway with you and I can see how somebody might think that's, you know, but who else is gonna do it, is kind of how I see it, so I gotta be the one, you know? It's a shitty job, actually. But you're so pathetic. So it's… it's more pity than friendship is how I see you, is the… the thing. I feel all this, you know, all this pity for you and I just think somebody should keep an eye on you. It's kinda like having a mentally challenged little brother.

(*Beat.*)

I just–

DANNY. Trev?

TREVOR. Yeah?

DANNY. Me too.

(*Beat.* **DANNY** *touches him.*)

OK?

TREVOR. OK.

DANNY. OK. Fuck! Hold on.

(**DANNY** *looks off.*)

Look at him.

(**TREVOR** *looks off.*)

I just think…

TREVOR. What?

DANNY. Wait.

(**DANNY** *takes out his cell and starts texting.*)

Shit. Goddamn…

TREVOR. Go a little–

DANNY. Will you shut up?

(**TREVOR** *reads what* **DANNY** *is writing.*)

TREVOR. Don't you fucking send that.

DANNY. Why?

(**TREVOR** *grabs the phone before* **DANNY** *can press send.*)

Hey!

TREVOR. Danny, you can't send a three word text to her that says "He's too African-y."

DANNY. C'mon…

(**DANNY** *tries to grab the phone back.*)

TREVOR. No, you can't.

(**TREVOR** *erases the text and hands the phone back to* **DANNY.**)

DANNY Jesus.

TREVOR. You're the writer. Find better words.

DANNY. I just mean he's so, you know…

TREVOR. What?

DANNY. He doesn't pass the, whatever, the paper bag–

TREVOR. Oh my god, you–

DANNY. I just mean he's… just that he's a little darker than I thought he should–

TREVOR. Dude, find better words.

DANNY. You know what I–

TREVOR. Danny.

DANNY. Right.

TREVOR. OK?

DANNY. OK.

(**DANNY** *starts to write another text.* **TREVOR**'s *phone rings with a text notification.* **TREVOR** *takes out his phone and reads it and laughs.*)

Who's that?

TREVOR. What?

DANNY. Who's on your–

TREVOR. Oh, nobody. Just work.

DANNY. Oh yeah?

TREVOR. It is.

DANNY. Uh-huh.

TREVOR. You know, we got some shit going down there, it's just work.

DANNY. You got a very demanding temp job.

TREVOR. Very.

DANNY. Uh-huh.

TREVOR. So…

DANNY. OK.

TREVOR. OK.

*(*TREVOR *and* DANNY *both turn away from each other and write their texts. They both hit send. Beat.)*

TREVOR. What'd you write?

DANNY. What'd *you* write?

TREVOR. I just told them I'd be there a little early. To fix the shit. At work.

DANNY. Oh.

TREVOR. What'd you write?

DANNY. Basically the same thing. Except that it wasn't about being early, or fixing any shit or going to work. But otherwise, basically it was the same.

(Beat.)

I said it better, OK?

TREVOR. You did?

DANNY. I swear. And I wasn't gonna send that other one.

TREVOR. Sure.

DANNY. I would never! Jesus.

TREVOR. OK.

DANNY. I'm not some… Hold on.

*(*DANNY *looks off)*

There goes another one.

*(*TREVOR *looks off. Beat.)*

Wow. Well, I hope *he's* good.

*(*DANNY *looks back at* TREVOR. TREVOR *stares at* DANNY.)*

(Blackout.)

Scene 7

(Danny and Pete's Apartment)

(TREVOR sits checking his cell phone while DANNY and PETE are moving in and out of the room, packing a suitcase around him. The script is on top of a small pile of to-be-packed clothes.)

PETE. Danny, is this the shirt?

DANNY. No, it's gonna be warm there. The stripey one.

PETE. In the wash.

DANNY. In the wash?

PETE. Yeah. You wore it two days ago. Did you think it took a bath all on its own?

DANNY. But I wanna take the stripey one.

TREVOR. They have, like, laundromats there, you know.

PETE. Have you ever seen him do laundry?

TREVOR. I must've.

PETE. You haven't.

DANNY. Sure he has.

TREVOR. Oh my god, I don't think I've ever seen it.

PETE. He's like the Dorian Gray of clean clothes. There's an attic somewhere out there with a handsome young man in an outfit that just gets filthier and filthier.

(PETE cuts off DANNY's response with a kiss.)

DANNY. Nice move.

PETE. Oh I got moves, babe.

(TREVOR's text notification rings. He checks his phone.)

DANNY. Who's calling?

TREVOR. Nobody. Text.

(He answers the text.)

What time's your flight?

DANNY. Ten or eleven or something in the morning.

PETE. She's at eight. He has to not be on her flight. It's all so spy-tastic. Here's the shirt.

DANNY. But it's all wrinkled.

PETE. Danny, so help me Krishna I'm gonna–

TREVOR. Pack the g.d. shirt.

DANNY. All right, jeez.

TREVOR. It's just–

(*His text notification rings. He checks his phone and laughs while typing a response.* **DANNY** *and* **PETE** *stare at him until he finishes and looks up at them.*)

What?

DANNY. You know, you can just talk to her on the phone in front of us.

TREVOR. Who?

PETE. Oh, please.

TREVOR. That was this guy from work, had a question about–

DANNY. Work has been a real bitch lately, huh?

TREVOR. It was!

PETE. We approve, Trevor. We like her.

TREVOR. Who?

DANNY. We like her.

TREVOR. Ah, shit. How long've you known?

DANNY. I dunno, like five minutes before you did.

TREVOR. Shit.

PETE. It was a little on the obvious side.

DANNY. She's awesome, Trev.

PETE. Will she hate that we know?

TREVOR. No. She thinks not telling you was bullshit. I just thought you'd be mad.

DANNY. Why the hell–?

TREVOR. It just seemed like I was moving in on your, whatever, territory.

PETE. You're nuts, white boy.

TREVOR. Yeah, yeah.

DANNY. Look, T, she's great, and a humonculous improvement on every single woman you've brought home since you and Crazy broke–

TREVOR. Shelby.

DANNY. Since you and crazy Shelby broke up. Emilie's great, she's smart, funny, we were just saying–

PETE. Oh, yeah, last night–

DANNY. *(sincerely)* You know, if nothing else, this whole thing has been great, we got a new friend. And bonus-round, we didn't have any black friends, so she's a two-for-one.

TREVOR. What?

DANNY. You know, everybody we know is so Euro-mutt. I was starting to feel like we were always gonna be this vanilla milk shake club, this–

PETE. You know what he means.

TREVOR. I guess…

DANNY. And you guys are super cute together. Like a sweet little Oreo cookie.

TREVOR. Dude…

DANNY. Oh, Jesus, wait a minute, I was joking. Can't I–

TREVOR. Not really.

DANNY. C'mon, it's just us, can't I–

TREVOR. It's kinda not–

    *(**TREVOR**'s phone buzzes.)*

PETE. Oh, for Christ's sake, give me the thing.

    *(He grabs **TREVOR**'s phone and dials.)*

    No, no. Sorry, it's Pete. Yeah. Yes, we sleuthed it all out. I know. He was an idiot. Let's hate him. OK. See you in a couple weeks. *(to **DANNY**)* She wants to talk to you.

    *(**DANNY** takes the phone.)*

DANNY. Hey, Em. Yeah. Uh-huh.

    *(He covers the receiver, to **PETE**.)*

    Where're those grey socks with the black stripe?

PETE. Danny, go in there and look in the drawer that is literally dedicated to your socks and dainties.

DANNY. You're beautiful, you know that?

PETE. I'm aware.

DANNY. *(back into the phone, as he exits)* I was thinking about moving that scene, but if it's too early, we'll have problems with the…

  (DANNY's gone.)

PETE. I have to tell you, when I pictured Danny getting one of his plays done, it didn't ever look much like this.

TREVOR. Dude, tell me about it.

PETE. I mean, I always thought the big decision would be whether or not to tell *Time* or *Newsweek* or whatever about *me*, not about whether my fucking boyfriend actually wrote the fucking thing or not. Not that I have an opinion about it or anything.

TREVOR. Petey–

PETE. It's OK. All good, right? This is what I get, I'm sure Mom will tell me, this is what I get for marrying a fucking artist. "He's so much more exciting than anybody I've ever met," I told her. I could've stayed with Doctor Barry Levine, heroic child periodontist two years ago, but no, no, I thought him being boring was the worst thing possible. That plus the great irony of his overbite.

TREVOR. You're full of it, you know? All this too-cool-for-my-relationship b.s.

PETE. Like you have a leg to stand–

TREVOR. All right, all right.

PETE. Look, I'm nuts for him, but this current episode of How Crazy Can I Be? is getting on my last nerve.

DANNY. *(off)* GODDAMN SHITBALLS.

PETE. The right side, under the belts–

DANNY. *(off)* I can't find–

PETE. Look under the– You need me to physically–?

DANNY. *(off)* OK, OK. Sorry, Mom.

PETE. See what I mean?

TREVOR. Sure. But this is all going to be over soon. And it's all going to work out.

PETE. Is it?

TREVOR. It is. Life, you know, it works out. It does. Danny's smart, Pete. He knows what he's doing.

PETE. I hate to break it to you, T-bird, but he has no idea what he's doing.

TREVOR. And she's smart, too. She wouldn't be doing this if–

PETE. OK. OK. Whatever you need to believe. But I'll just say I'm... leery, that's all I'm gonna say. I'm leery. My boyfriend's smartnitude to one side and your girlfriend's–

TREVOR. Hold on–

PETE. Whatever she is, your girlfriend, your lovah–

TREVOR. Jesus.

PETE. Your lovah's to the other side, no matter how smart anybody is, wherever you step, big ol' emotional-type land mines... boom, boom... you know?

TREVOR. Everything worthwhile is, man.

PETE. Boy, I wish I had gone to drama school. You all came out believing the weirdest shit.

DANNY. *(Re-entering empty-handed. To **PETE**.)*
Babe, they weren't there.

*(**DANNY** hands the phone to **TREVOR**.)*

She wants to talk to you.

TREVOR. Hello. Hi. Yes. I know. I know! You can, you know, like totally punish me if you want.

DANNY. OK.

PETE. Gawd.

TREVOR. Yeah. Like, half an hour. Yeah. OK. I will.

(He hangs up.)

She says bye.

PETE. Yeah. That's what she said.

TREVOR. *(getting his things together)* So, safe flight, blah blah blah, all that. See you in a couple weeks, brother.

DANNY. Can you believe this shit?

TREVOR. This shit cannot be believed. Peabody, see you there.

PETE. Watch your step. Boom, boom.

DANNY. What does that–

TREVOR. Nothing. He doesn't–

PETE. Private joke. See you there.

TREVOR. Later, boys.

(TREVOR *exits.*)

DANNY. What was that–

PETE. Nothing.

DANNY. Pete.

PETE. Nothing you don't know. Just getting my... whatever, my hesitations out about this plan you and Trevor's sweet chocolate treat have cooked up.

DANNY. It's my plan, baby.

PETE. Weren't you just discussing scene placement with the help when you were trying to find your lucky socks?

DANNY. It's my play.

PETE. OK.

DANNY. It is.

PETE. OK.

DANNY. She's going into rehearsals in two days, going in there alone in two days. She's... I dunno, she may be on the team, but it's mine.

PETE. Right.

DANNY. She's the conduit. That's all.

PETE. Gotcha.

DANNY. She is.

PETE. No, I understand. You're Captain Kirk and she's your communications officer. She's Lieutenant Uhura.

Pretty little mini-skirted red-shirt lieutenant. And we all know what happens to the red-shirts on that show, right?

DANNY. What?

PETE. They die, Danny. They die.

(*PETE kisses **DANNY** and exits.*)

DANNY. And why can you get all "sweet chocolate treat" but I can't even–

PETE. *(off)* Jesus, Danny, because he likes her now, you know?

DANNY. Yeah, but–

PETE. *(off)* You're Mr. Theatre. Know your fuckin' audience, babe.

DANNY. Right.

(*PETE re-enters with **DANNY**'s socks. Beat.*)

PETE. Hey.

DANNY. Yeah?

PETE. I'm so proud of you it makes my toenails hurt, you know?

DANNY. I know.

PETE. Good.

(*PETE holds up the socks.*)

For the record? Under the belts.

(*PETE packs the socks.*)

DANNY. Uhura didn't die, you know.

PETE. They would never have killed a black woman on that ridiculous liberal space opera, Danny. In the real world? They get butchered all the time. Just sayin'.

(*He exits. Blackout.*)

Scene 8a

(Danny's Hotel Room/Emilie's Hotel Room)

(DANNY and EMILIE are on the phone. They each have a copy of the script in hand.)

DANNY. He said that?

EMILIE. Maybe five minutes after they cleared the donut tray from the meet-and-greet.

DANNY. And you–

EMILIE. What was I supposed to do? I said thank you. I don't know. I didn't know what to say.

DANNY. Lorraine Hansberry? No way.

EMILIE. "Our next Lorraine." Which is worse. As if she didn't need a last name to identify her.

DANNY. Yikes.

EMILIE. And I just stood there, kinda–

DANNY. God, I wish I–

EMILIE. I know, I know.

DANNY. You know?

EMILIE. I do.

DANNY. Then what?

EMILIE. The read-thru was good. And then L Jay–

DANNY. L-Jay?

EMILIE. Lawrence.

DANNY. You call Lawrence James L-Jay? Not Larry? Not Mr. James? L-Jay?

EMILIE. Yeah…

DANNY. Seriously?

EMILIE. Seriously.

DANNY. Why did I not know that? I've never heard that.

EMILIE. He said it's kind of an in-the-room thing.

DANNY. You mean an in-the-black-room thing.

EMILIE. Maybe…

DANNY. I just mean, whatever. That would never have happened if I'd been there. Because that's never been in an interview, that's never been in the press. He was on Charlie Rose and Charlie called him Larry the whole hour.

EMILIE. I dunno, Danny. That seems a little–

DANNY. Call me D-Lar, please. I think I wanna be D-Lar from now on. And you can be E-May. Or E-Mar. What's Martin? May or Mar?

EMILIE. I have no idea. But there's no way to say what would've happened because you're not the girl in the fuckin' room, right? I am.

DANNY. Um... You are. Yes.

EMILIE. So I think playing the if-I-had-been-in-the-room game is a loser from square one, and I also think, just so I've said it, any phrase like "in-the-black-room" is probably not the best way for you and me to be talking. For reasons that seem so obvious I can't believe I have to say it.

DANNY. Fair enough. Sorry, I got carried away.

EMILIE. You sure did.

(Beat.)

Look, Danny, I think you're gonna be thrilled about this. They are all kind of amazing.

DANNY. Was it weird with what's-his-name?

EMILIE. Kevin?

DANNY. Yeah, was it–

EMILIE. Nah. We did that show together three, four years ago. He barely remembered me. I mean he did, but only in the way where he was all, "I can't believe you wrote a play, girl." And I was kind of, "Believe it bitch."

DANNY. How'd the new–?

EMILIE. Great.

DANNY. The new shit–?

EMILIE. Really great.

DANNY. Oh my god, I wanna be there!

EMILIE. I know, I know. Look, Mr. James–

DANNY. L-Jay.

EMILIE. I'm gonna go with Mr. James from now on if you don't mind.

DANNY. All right, all right.

EMILIE. He said he has a couple thoughts.

DANNY. Such as?

EMILIE. I dunno. That's all he said. "A couple thoughts."

DANNY. OK.

EMILIE. It's called collaboration, you moron.

DANNY. I just–

EMILIE. Danny, we can handle this, OK?

DANNY. I said OK!

EMILIE. Oh, and get this. After the first performance? There's a speech.

DANNY. What?

EMILIE. The playwright makes a speech. To the friggin' audience. So…

DANNY. So there's a speech.

EMILIE. Yeah.

DANNY. To introduce the playwright?

EMILIE. Uh-huh.

DANNY. So that'll be…

EMILIE. Yeah…

(*Beat.*)

DANNY. I think I just pooped myself a little.

EMILIE. Awesome.

(*Blackout.*)

Scene 8b

(Emilie's Hotel Room/A Coffee Chain)

(EMILIE and TREVOR are on their cellphones, EMILIE in warmer weather clothes, TREVOR not so much. EMILIE is absently paging through the script.)

TREVOR. I'm kind of not so much at home, you know.

EMILIE. I know.

TREVOR. So stop it.

EMILIE. C'mon.

TREVOR. No.

EMILIE. C'mon.

TREVOR. Nooooo. There's, like, human beings two feet from me. Lots of human beings all around me.

EMILIE. Chicken.

TREVOR. No shit.

(Beat.)

More about today, please.

EMILIE. I'm so, so, so tired of having phone conversations about this friggin' play. I keep asking Danny to meet me at some diner and he's terrified. As if we couldn't just be friends. As if he couldn't just be here to support me. Or see me. Or whatever.

TREVOR. Em, you still got a couple weeks there. If anybody saw him there, anybody who knows him–

EMILIE. Who knows him?

TREVOR. That's not fair. There are people in that community–

EMILIE. My community.

TREVOR. Your community who know him.

EMILIE. I doubt that.

TREVOR. I mean your theatrical community.

EMILIE. What the fuck is that supposed to mean?

TREVOR. I mean that world there, that festival is full of people and some of them might know him.

EMILIE. Oh. I thought you meant–

TREVOR. I know what you thought.

EMILIE. Oh.

TREVOR. You know I didn't mean that.

EMILIE. I know.

TREVOR. I'd never mean that.

EMILIE. Danny would.

TREVOR. Danny's Danny.

EMILIE. Yes he is.

TREVOR. And what's *that*–

EMILIE. No, no, sorry. I'm sorry. It's all good. I'm just...

> (**EMILIE** *takes a quick dirty picture of herself. She sends it to* **TREVOR**. *His phone buzzes. He looks at the picture. He groans.*)

Jesus, I think I'm just horny. You know?

TREVOR. Join the effin' club.

> (*Beat.*)

So, rehearsal?

EMILIE. OK. Truth?

TREVOR. Always.

EMILIE. It's so fucking exciting I can't even begin to tell you. And sometimes when I start to tell Danny–

TREVOR. Did he try to make you call him D-Lar?

EMILIE. I do not wanna talk about the D-Lar Incident.

TREVOR. Sorry. You were saying–

EMILIE. Um... When I try to tell Danny how exciting, how unbelievable it is he gets all–

TREVOR. Sulky.

EMILIE. Oh my god, like I took his Hot Wheels away.

TREVOR. That's m'boy.

EMILIE. It's infuriating.

TREVOR. Well, you know, from his–

EMILIE. Yeah, yeah, yeah, I know. But this is *exactly* the bed he made, so he can just suck it up, put his little bleached bung in the air and bite his pillow. Right?

TREVOR. I kinda think that's not the best–

EMILIE. Because just to be in that room, where they are all tearin' this motherfucker up, I can't believe it. I'm almost jealous.

TREVOR. Of them?

EMILIE. Of me, I think. Like I'm not even there.

TREVOR. Because you're kinda not.

(*Beat.*)

EMILIE. Yeah. Because of that. And then I come back here and try to remember every single detail, every single moment, so Danny can feel like he's there, because he's not, and I take his notes, and I wait for you to call, and another day is gone.

TREVOR. You just want it all to be over.

EMILIE. Maybe. What I really want is to have maybe one moment in the not-too-far-away future where I feel like everything isn't about to blow up in my face.

TREVOR. Well, then, that makes three of us.

EMILIE. Three? Oh, you, me, and your little butt buddy?

TREVOR. Emilie Martin!

EMILIE. What?

TREVOR. That's–

EMILIE. Whatever.

TREVOR. It's not what grown people say.

EMILIE. Jesus, Trevor.

TREVOR. It's not what grown people I sleep with say.

EMILIE. OK.

TREVOR. You shouldn't be so hard on him, you know?

EMILIE. Hey, no offense, but you're not even close to objective about him.

TREVOR. I'm not?

EMILIE. No way. You're his fuckin' muse for Christ's sake.

TREVOR. Well, that's disturbing.

EMILIE. You don't think the guy's, like, completely in love with you?

TREVOR. OK, what?

EMILIE. 'Cuz he is.

TREVOR. Oh, please.

EMILIE. Trev–

TREVOR. Just stop, OK?

EMILIE. He–

TREVOR. Really. Stop. That's some tiny bullshit. You can just be friends with somebody and not be, like, in love with them, you know.

EMILIE. Maybe, but I don't have any straight guy friends. Not really. Penises have fuckin' agendas.

TREVOR. You know what? My plan is to stick around while you work your shit out, 'cuz you got a little shit workin' to do. So enough. I'm done with this. Because the thing is I, you know... love you... a little.

EMILIE. Trev–

TREVOR. Just a little. Get over it. And it seems to me you got some high school views on people and you should totally aim higher.

EMILIE. But he–

TREVOR. I'm talking to you now, OK?

EMILIE. I dunno.

TREVOR. Nine more days.

EMILIE. I know.

TREVOR. Home stretch.

EMILIE. Yeah, yeah.

TREVOR. Em, you are majorly stressed, OK? You both are.

EMILIE. But he–

TREVOR. Look, why don't you go make a little bath, put some girl stuff in it, and let me tell you some things.

Some things about what I might like to do with, you know, like my fingers, my tongue, stuff like that.

EMILIE. Trev...

TREVOR. Stuff my fingers, my tongue, other parts of me, stuff they might like to do to you. When you get outta that tub. When you're all naked and shiny and mine.

EMILIE. Yours? When I'm–?

TREVOR. You know what I–

EMILIE. Jesus, that's exactly what–

TREVOR. Em?

EMILIE. Yeah?

TREVOR. Be quiet and lay down. OK? 'Cuz here I come.

EMILIE. Oh, shit. What about the human beings all around you?

TREVOR. Fuck 'em.

(Blackout.)

Scene 8c

(Danny's Hotel Room/Emilie's Hotel Room)

(DANNY and EMILIE are on the phone. DANNY is furiously waving the script around.)

DANNY. Absolutely not.

EMILIE. Danny.

DANNY. Absofuckinglutely not.

EMILIE. C'mon.

DANNY. No. No. No.

EMILIE. It's a good idea.

DANNY. It's no idea. It's not an idea. It's censorship, maybe. That's one word to describe it. But not idea. It's there–

EMILIE. Censorship?

DANNY. It's there for a reason.

EMILIE. So cut it for a reason. Or at least tone it down. Turns out some people find it offensive.

DANNY. No shit. That's why it's there.

EMILIE. What?

DANNY. I mean, it's there because it's the way people talk. I hear it every day. You hear it every day.

EMILIE. What's that sup–

DANNY. I mean everybody hears it every day. Please don't get all hyper-prickly over this. It's there for a fucking reason. Besides, what's the big deal, Emilie? It's not like it's the first time you've ever heard it.

EMILIE. Look, it's not my favorite word, I'll be honest, but just because I'm telling you doesn't mean it's me. There's a director here. There's some dramaturg/producer liaison in the room the whole time. I've been told there's an audience to consider. So I'm telling you. And it's all over that scene. It seems like it's every other word.

DANNY. Because that is how people fucking talk. They say it. They call each other nig–

EMILIE. Don't.

DANNY. They do.

EMILIE. I know, but we're not gonna say it. You and me? We're not gonna.

DANNY. You know, just because people hate the word, doesn't mean I like it. I'm terrified of it. But it's just a word, you know?

EMILIE. That's–

DANNY. It's just one fuckin' word. It doesn't mean anything unless you *want* it to.

EMILIE. Not that word.

DANNY. Especially that word. It's only a bullet if you load the gun with it. Otherwise it has no... value. It's just letters and sounds.

EMILIE. That's pretty fuckin' convenient.

DANNY. The world is a place that gets described by the words we create, the ways we put those words together to help ourselves and to, you know, hurt each other.

But they are just words, and I'm done talking about this. You're not the only one with words you don't like to hear.

EMILIE. Oh, please.

DANNY. You know what? I got words too.

EMILIE. It's not the same.

DANNY. Emilie, it's exactly, exactly the same. I never use *my* word. Never.

EMILIE. *(imitating him)* "I never use *my* word." But it's OK for me to say fag–

DANNY. No. No. Emilie, I know you're sick of this, but that word is the same to me. To me, that word is the same. To me.

EMILIE. And if I write some play about these four white gay guys?

DANNY. I can't wait to read it.

EMILIE. Danny, it's a big deal because a white guy wrote this play, and that changes things.

DANNY. Nobody fucking knows that!

EMILIE. *I* know it.

DANNY. So?

EMILIE. So it matters. Because if a white guy decides to use that–

DANNY. Bullshit.

EMILIE. to use it, it's a choice. If I say it, or if I hear it in, whatever, my life, it's not the same.

DANNY. Bullshit, bullshit.

EMILIE. Well, then just cut it back.

DANNY. Nope.

EMILIE. *(imitating him)* "Bullshit, bullshit–"

DANNY. Dammit, stop making fun of the way I talk. I kind of fucking hate that.

EMILIE. Sorry, but you–

DANNY. And besides, it's different! It's goddamn different because it's in a fucking play, Emilie. Because I chose

to put it in the fucking play because that is the way
they talk, and it's in the–

EMILIE. They? They? The way *they* talk?

DANNY. Don't make this something else.

EMILIE. Look, maybe I'm a, you know, maybe I'm... I mean
I'm taking a paycheck for all of this. I get it. But this is
bullshit. This is–

DANNY. It's not bullshit. It's just true.

EMILIE. I have a responsibility, Danny.

DANNY. To me.

EMILIE. I have a responsibility to be on the lookout, to
watch for things that could be damaging, in life, in
my life, I have a responsibility. Just like you. And I'm
looking out for those things right now. And you talk
like you're staging a cultural revolution here. It's just
a play festival, Danny, a festival of *plays*, and nobody
gives a shit about any play, let alone this play, and I'm
telling you that in the relative safety of this artistic
what-do-you-call-it, enclave–

DANNY. Conclave, actually.

EMILIE. Goddammit, Danny–

DANNY. Sorry.

EMILIE. Jesus. This smart guy who has experience and
talent has ideas about making your play better and I'm
bringing those ideas to you because that's the fucked-
up smoke signal system you set up, *you* set it up, and
you can decide what you want to do with all of it, but
yelling at me, ordering me around, telling me what I
am and am not going to do is not going to be part
of that fucking equation anymore. Not anymore. Or
you can deal with what it might be if I walk out of that
room and then you won't even have a play in a festival
anymore, because you'll just be shit out of luck.

DANNY. Emilie, with all due respect–

EMILIE. Or no respect–

DANNY. With all due fucking respect, you are getting paid
to look out for me. You are getting paid delicious cash
money to look out for my play. Not your feelings. Or
your history. Or whatever. Your people. For me.

EMILIE. My people? My people? Goddamn, Danny.

DANNY. You know what I–

EMILIE. It's in the scene thirty-seven times, Danny. That's
thirty-seven times that everybody jumps in their seat a
little bit, thirty-seven times you can scan the audience
to see who notices and who doesn't, thirty-seven times
the... the... Fuck!

(Beat.)

It's excessive and pornographic. And it's the only scene
we're talking about, because it's so frequent there.

DANNY. No, it's because that's the scene you worked on
today. You weed it out there, and soon it'll be out of
the play, and then it won't be a play, it'll just be a movie
of the week, because it'll have all the teeth of a tod-
dler and it might as well be your name on it, because
I won't care. And not for nothin', but you didn't have
problem number one with any fuckin' words 'til you
found yourself hip-deep in that room, so–

EMILIE. Oh my god, that's–

DANNY. And, and, and this might seem like something you
don't care about, but I'll sue you.

EMILIE. What?

DANNY. And your director friend. And I'll eventually
win. I will. I will be that douchebag who hires some
chumsucking ambulance-stalking advertises-on-the-
fucking-subway-lower-than-a-cataract lawyer and follow
you to your last breath and your shallow anonymous
grave. So don't do it. Just drop it. Just let it go. And
tell Lawrence the Tony Winning L-Jay James to fucking
drop it too. Because that is what you're getting paid
for and that is the end of fucking that. Your responsibility. Bullshit.

(He hangs up.)

FUCK!

EMILIE. FUCK!

(Blackout.)

Scene 8d

(A Coffee Chain)

(March. No jackets. PETE *and* TREVOR *are sitting side by side, facing a window.* PETE *has the script and other papers in front of him [or on his lap].)*

PETE. This place is so depressing.

TREVOR. It looks like all the others.

PETE. I mean this town.

TREVOR. Oh.

PETE. Of course *this* place is depressing.

TREVOR. The town seems like a lot of towns. It's a lot like this place.

PETE. I was getting food last night at the Kwik-E-Mart or whatever the hell it is–

TREVOR. On-the-Run.

PETE. For real?

TREVOR. I shit you not.

PETE. Jesus. At the On-the-Run and this dirty little kid said to his fat mother–

TREVOR. You're kind of the milk of human kindness, aren't you?

PETE. He said he wanted to look at the shopping list, and his mom gave him a piece of paper from her purse and the little boy looked at it and said, "Mommy, what's this?" and she looked at it and said, "Oh, sorry, that's my suicide note" and took it back.

TREVOR. That didn't happen.

PETE. It should've.

(Beat.)

TREVOR. You know, you're from a town not much bigger than this.

PETE. We all are. That's what cities are built of, people like you and me who needed a bigger place to hate.

TREVOR. How's Danny? I can't tell from the phone.

PETE. I can't tell from not the phone. He's a mess, kinda. Nauseous-like, awake all the– He wandered the lobby of the festival today.

TREVOR. He left the cave?

PETE. Yup.

TREVOR. No way.

PETE. Alert the media. How's Emilie?

TREVOR. Good. She's sorta having a blast, I think. It was cool to get on the set today, she said.

PETE. They get so spatty. It's really fuckin' with his state of–

TREVOR. I know, but–

PETE. Oh, shit. Here's the new complete thing.

(**PETE** *gives* **TREVOR** *the script.*)

Danny says the changes they asked for are underlined or double underlined or whatever. He says they'll know.

TREVOR. You know, he coulda just emailed this.

PETE. He did.

TREVOR. They why print this–

PETE. 'Cuz he wanted to make extra sure it–

TREVOR. It's such a waste of–

PETE. It's the only way he can–

TREVOR. This is bad for the trees, you know?

PETE. Listen, Lorax, he… Jesus. Because he's crazy right now, Trev. OK? He's–

TREVOR. OK. I know. Four more days. That's what I keep telling her. Four more days. It's good we're here now, I think. Gives everybody a pressure-type release valve situation.

PETE. Sure.

TREVOR. But she's wound pretty tight, and as eff-ed up and slightly exciting as I thought this plan was, I'm pretty much on the side of just plain eff-ed up now.

PETE. Amen to the fucked up.

TREVOR. I mean, this will be over and we'll go back to normal, right?

PETE. I don't even know what that means anymore.

(Beat.)

Here.

(PETE hands another sheet to TREVOR.)

TREVOR. What's this?

PETE. It's the speech.

TREVOR. What speech?

PETE. The speech Danny wrote for her.

TREVOR. For the play? I thought the changes were all underlined or–

PETE. For Emilie.

TREVOR. What the... the what?

PETE. The speech he wrote for her for at the first–

TREVOR. He wrote her a speech?

PETE. Yup.

TREVOR. Dude.

PETE. Yup.

TREVOR. She is completely, you know, capable of introducing him in a non-humiliating way.

PETE. Of course she is.

TREVOR. She's gonna have an opinion about this.

PETE. He said something like, "Well, she's an actress, isn't she?"

TREVOR. Pete...

PETE. Actually that's exactly what he said.

(TREVOR begins to read the speech.)

TREVOR. Oh Christ.

PETE. So maybe let's just put that whole "back to normal" thing on hold for a little bit, don't you think?

(Blackout.)

Scene 8e

(The Same Coffee Chain)

*(**DANNY** and **EMILIE**, both dressed up. She is holding the script and some flowers.)*

EMILIE. They're nice.

DANNY. Pete found 'em at the grocery store. He is spending way too much time there.

EMILIE. The grocery store?

DANNY. Like he's writing a thesis on it.

EMILIE. Anyway. Thanks.

DANNY. You're welcome.

(Beat.)

By the way, I'm completely freaked out.

EMILIE. I know.

DANNY. You aren't?

EMILIE. Oh, I am.

DANNY. Good.

(Beat.)

Sorry I was a dick a couple times there.

EMILIE. One or two.

DANNY. Sorry.

EMILIE. Or three, or nine, or sixty-sev–

DANNY. We got through it.

EMILIE. Yeah, we got through it.

DANNY. How was the dress today?

EMILIE. Oh, it was awesome.

DANNY. I kinda can't get over the fact that I haven't even seen it.

EMILIE. Danny, honestly you're gonna be blown away. It's maybe the best thing I've ever seen.

DANNY. Don't. Please. I get a little panicky.

EMILIE. Well, it is.

DANNY. Whatever angina is, I think I have it. Or asthma. Or some "a" disease. Something that makes you kind of pant or whatever.

EMILIE. You're going to be fine.

DANNY. I hope so.

EMILIE. You are.

(Beat.)

DANNY. Did you memorize the thing?

EMILIE. Your fuckin' speech?

DANNY. Well, your fuckin' speech.

EMILIE. I did. I wish you'd just let me talk. I feel so...

DANNY. Please, Em.

EMILIE. Jesus...

DANNY. Just–

EMILIE. "Given this play, given its people..." That whole "crossroads of inspiration and despair" intro, the "but-I-have-something-to-tell-you-I-didn't-write-this-play" melodrama of it.

DANNY. It needs to sound–

EMILIE. Pretentious.

DANNY. Written.

EMILIE. But I don't wanna make an ass of myself, you know?

DANNY. You won't.

EMILIE. It's–

DANNY. Em, you won't. They're gonna be so... like... OK, I don't know what anybody's gonna be.

EMILIE. It just makes me so fucking nervous.

DANNY. Ditto. But it was the whole deal, right?

EMILIE. I guess.

DANNY. And tomorrow we can start just being friends. I'm totally not sorry to see this phase of us go away.

EMILIE. Oh, no. Not sorry.

DANNY. Nope.

EMILIE. Not sorry at all.

   (Beat.)

DANNY. Emilie?

EMILIE. Yeah?

DANNY. Break a leg.

EMILIE. OK.

   (Beat.)

DANNY. Break a leg.

   (Blackout.)

Scene 9

(A Microphone)

*(**EMILIE** stands in a spotlight, holding the script.)*

EMILIE. Thank you. Thank you so much. This is... God, I can't believe how nervous I am.

(Beat.)

OK. First off, I have to thank Barry Thompson and the entire staff here, not only because they were smart enough to pick this play, but for the past four weeks, which have been full of some of the most exciting days I've had in the theatre. And to Mr. James, yeah, I know, L-Jay, and the cast: Kevin, Susie, Amy, Marcus, you can't imagine what it's been like to sit and watch you spin your magic because you were too busy spinning it. But I'm in awe. So take that. You have my awe.

(Beat.)

OK. Now. Given this play, given its people and its location, its life, its spark, having lived with these characters at this... at this crossroads... this crossroads of inspiration and... and...

(Beat.)

All right. I don't know about you, but I'm gonna come right out and say it. I think this play is the fuckin' bomb. Straight up. The bomb. And maybe it's just a play, but... You know what? That's not even it. I mean, that's bullshit, that brand of minimizing the... the experience. And I'm talking to you. That's right. You. Because I was sitting there too and I thought it was good and all, but this... this story matters. And I thought it was all about *who* tells it, but that's not... It's not about the owning. That would be the easy way out. It's about the telling itself. Life is too... almost gone before you've lived it to not stand up and say, "This is what happened; this is what I know to be." And I know we all want to own our story. That's just how it is to be a person. But tonight is not about that. Not about mine or yours. Tonight is about the... the inevitable passing on of it. Now it's out there, it's... it's not going to be yours anymore. Or even mine. We're better than that. The higher road, the better path, is letting the story go do its job. And that's what I didn't know before tonight. That's what I wasn't paying attention to. We don't pay attention to it. I think we... we go to our football games and watch our TVs and eat our fuckin' hot dogs and try so so hard to ignore our responsibility. But tonight, here, now, we can... we can make this story matter. Make a difference. What we tell can make a... All of us. Not you. Not me. All of us. It's not a sentiment. It's an opportunity. I wanted to get up here tonight and say what I meant. Because it matters. This play matters. And I'm just so proud to be here, so proud to be a part of this and so happy that you all got to hear me say in my own words what I meant.

(Beat.)

Damn. I guess that wasn't so hard after all. Was it?

(Blackout.)

Scene 10

(Danny's Hotel Room)

*(**DANNY** and **EMILIE** are staring at each other. The script is on the coffee table. There is a long moment where all four are almost frozen before **TREVOR** speaks.)*

TREVOR. Look...

DANNY. Shut up, Trev.

TREVOR. I think you should let her–

DANNY. I'm not kidding.

TREVOR. Danny, let her just–

PETE. Trev, I think–

TREVOR. OK. OK.

(Beat.)

DANNY. Do you have an answer for that?

(Beat.)

Emilie? Do you at least have a fucking answer for that?

EMILIE. We're not gonna get through this if you don't stop pissing at me.

DANNY. Oh god. Oh, I'm sorry. Please. Please forgive me. Please. Jesus Christ.

EMILIE. I'm not kidding.

DANNY. I AM NOT KIDDING EITHER. I AM NOT FUCKING KIDDING EITHER, EMILIE.

PETE. Danny.

DANNY. Fuck. OK. Sorry. I'm sorry.

DANNY. *(cont.)* I cannot   **PETE.** Babe. Babe.
fucking believe I'm
apologizing, but I'll try.

(Beat.)

TREVOR. Em, give him a break. Don't cut–

EMILIE. You'd best not help.

(Beat.)

OK?

(*Beat.*)

OK, Trevor?

TREVOR. I heard you.

EMILIE. Good. I don't have an answer, Danny. I told you, I didn't plan it.

DANNY. That's literally impossible for me to believe.

EMILIE. Fine. Believe what you want.

DANNY. I want credit for my goddamn play, Emilie. That's what I want. Believing you takes a far-back third or ninety-seventh place. It's my play!

EMILIE. I know. I know. I meant to do it. Like we planned. But I got up there, and I... Christ... I saw you sitting there, like a puppy ready to grab his bone.

EMILIE. (*cont.*) I looked at you and you were kind of glowing, and I got... furious. And I was so excited about the... I just... I just started talking.

PETE. Can you believe this?

PETE. The problem is you didn't stop talking, I think.

EMILIE. I'm not very interested in what you have to say about it, so you can just shut up, Pete, OK?

PETE. This is ridiculous.

(*He exits. Offstage:*)

Ahhh, Jesus, I am so fucking sick of theatre! Fucking theatre people! Fucking plays! Fucking play festivals! Motherfucking actors with their fucker fucking fuck fuck FUUUUUUCCCCCCKKKKK!!!!

(*He re-enters. Calmly.*)

Sorry. I just needed to–

DANNY. Babe.

PETE. Sorry. Jesus.

DANNY. Emilie. Em. I'm talking calmly now. I'm breathing. I'm not yelling. I swear.

EMILIE. OK.

DANNY. Look, I'm sorry I snapped at you a couple of times while we were working on it. I am. But I didn't mean it.

DANNY. *(cont.)* I was under a lot of, you know… A lot. And I was completely unprepared for how much it would kill me, one cut at a time, to not be there.

EMILIE. No, I know you didn't mean–

EMILIE. I know, Danny, but it was your plan. It went down exactly the way you wanted.

DANNY. You were there too, OK?

EMILIE. I know, I know. It's hard to–

DANNY. I get it. I get it. I put you in an impossible position. I see that now. From the get-go. It was a no-good place for you to be. It wasn't fair, and I thought it would be all about money. Or whatever. I thought an out-of-work actor would happy to, you know.

DANNY. *(cont.)* No, I mean, I'm saying it's not, you know, it's not OK, but I thought just getting to be a part of it would be enough for her. *(to EMILIE)* For you.

TREVOR. Stop, stop, let her–

EMILIE. Excuse me?

DANNY. I don't, I'm sorry, I don't do so well off-the-cuff. OK? I get a little… Listen.

(Beat.)

Listen. I didn't factor you in as a person. I see that now.

EMILIE. Ah.

DANNY. I see that from the very start I was thinking of you as, I don't know, an employee or something, and that's not right.

TREVOR. Hey, hey, Danny, you don't have to–

TREVOR. *(cont.)* He doesn't have to–	DANNY. No, Trev, I get it. And I get how you could be, whatever, pissed off by my glow, but you took my play away.

DANNY. *(cont.)* You took it. And I didn't think you were that person. Or I never would've hired you. And you said you were a whore–

EMILIE. I never–

DANNY. but that's not what I thought. I thought I had a new friend. Right? I told Trevor, right, Trev?

TREVOR. What?

DANNY. I told him. We both have been so happy to have you around, a new person in our, whatever, our thingie, our circle. It's been awesome. So however it started, and I admit fully I wasn't thinking when it started, I admit it, but however it started, whether I thought I was hiring a whatever-you-called-it, a puppet, a servant, a playwright's slave or whatev–

EMILIE. What the fuck...?

DANNY. No, no, no, that's not what I–

PETE. Danny, baby, you need to stop talk–

TREVOR. No shit.

DANNY No. Wait. Wait.

EMILIE. You know what? That's the problem. That's the thing, right there.

DANNY. What?

EMILE. That. You got yourself some real troubles dealing with people who are not like you, Danny, and I am all done.

(She starts to exit. To TREVOR*)*

You see? Now do you see what I–?

DANNY. Emilie, don't–

EMILIE. Don't what, Danny? Don't go? Don't what? Don't give my opinion? Don't say what I think? Don't take credit for you? Don't what? You got a lot of don'ts for the black girl you got in your employ.

DANNY. That's not fair.   **PETE.** Christ.

EMILIE. Fair or true?

DANNY. Not fucking fair! Not fucking both. You're twisting–

EMILIE. No. No, I'm actually just repeating what you said. And if you think I haven't noticed all along–

DANNY. Oh, please.

EMILIE. Fuck you, Danny. *(to* **TREVOR***)* You see it now? Huh? You listening to him?

TREVOR. Yeah, but I–

EMILIE. Or are you part of this lily white camp meeting mentality here?

TREVOR. Watch it, Em.

EMILIE. Are you?

DANNY. Answer her, T. Go ahead.

TREVOR. Shut up, Danny.

DANNY. Please, I wanna hear.

TREVOR. No. Because even if she's right, even if you're right, I only lose if I answer that, and I prefer to not lose, if you don't fucking mind. OK?

EMILIE. Whatever.

TREVOR. Whatever is right.

EMILIE. *(to* **DANNY***)* You know, you can keep playing "not it" here, but treating me like I don't have some, you know, some reason to feel a little like–

DANNY. Here's the thing, though, Em. Not one single thing was different from what I told you it would be. Not one.

EMILIE. Well...

DANNY. Not one fucking thing!

EMILIE. You know what's really crazy here? I loved it. I loved being in the… being part of it. It's sick. And the sad part is I don't even think, end of the day, I don't think you care about the play, really.

DANNY. Are you fucking–

EMILIE. Not really. I mean you do, but the reason you're having your pissy little tantrum is you didn't get your bullshit moment in the spotlight. **DANNY**. Pissy! **PETE**. This is such a load–

DANNY. I'm gonna–

EMILIE. It's not about the play. It's all about you.

DANNY. It's *only* about the play.

EMILIE. It was never about the play. It was all about Danny. Forget about me. Forget about my, you know, my career, my friends, the things I put on hold, at risk for your play, because I love the thing. Forget about Pete. And Trevor. About the 25 or 50 people who killed themselves to get your play going. It's always about Danny.

DANNY. And your selfless little act for 25% of all future profits makes you some kind of saint?

EMILIE. It makes me fucking practical.

DANNY. That's not all it makes you.

EMILIE. It might've been a little helpful if you'd filled me in on the fact that you were some big old racist shithead before we started.

PETE. Jesus Chr–

EMILIE. Because that mighta made me take a second look at all this.

PETE. Who isn't? You know? Jesus, you–

TREVOR. Em, you need to–

DANNY. No, no. I wanna hear this. Please. Let's say I am, let's say I'm the white-hoodiest cross-burner that ever was.

PETE. Are you kidding?

DANNY. No, let's say it's true. Because you still said yes. You still said, "OK, Mr. Closet Skinhead, I'll do it. I'll let myself–"

EMILIE. Are you fucking crazy?

DANNY. Shut up. You said yes. Because I didn't lie to you. I said it from the start. I'm probably the whitest dude I know, and I needed you to be the face on this, I needed you to legitimize this in the least up-front way in the history of not-smart ideas and you said yes. You said yes, Emilie. You said it.

EMILIE. BECAUSE I LOVE YOUR FUCKING PLAY, YOU ASSHOLE!

DANNY. You mean your play.

EMILIE. Fuck off. And I'm not gonna apologize for loving it. It's great. I still don't know how, but those people were screaming for it. They were on their feet for what felt like 3 years.

DANNY. I was there! It was–

(DANNY's *cell phone [which is not in his pocket] rings.*)

TREVOR. Oh, shit, is that–

DANNY. It's mine. *(to* EMILIE*)* You can't–

PETE. I'll–

DANNY. Leave it.

(ring)

EMILIE. You can answer it, I don't–

DANNY. Leave it, goddamit!

PETE. Jesus, OK. Don't be a–

(ring)

TREVOR. Danny, you should answer that, you should–

DANNY. For fuck's sake, let it go!

TREVOR. OK. Fine.

(It rings twice more while they listen. Beat.)

PETE. Both of you are pathetic here.

DANNY. She can't just–

PETE. Oh, please. You are both full of shit. Sorry, babe, but you are. You were a chickenshit to not stand behind the thing from the beginning, you know you–

DANNY. I couldn't!

PETE. Uh-huh. People can decide what to do, you know, Danny. I love you, but people have whole choices in front of them when they get up in the morning. You don't think Björk had a back-up outfit when she put that fucking swan thing on before walking the red carpet? I mean, really. *(to* EMILIE*)* And you. Seems like a crazy time to be flying your big bold Liberian flag here.

TREVOR. Oh my god.

PETE. I mean it. I think you expected him to be in some future tense seeing how this was all gonna turn out, but it doesn't take a call to the psychic hotline to get that this was always A TERRIBLE IDEA. So don't get mad at Danny for the wheels coming off. You think he's the white devil? Him? Oh, please. He's a fucking kitten.

EMILIE. A fluffy little white one.

PETE. Jesus, Emilie, is it your first day on the planet?

EMILIE. You know you're a perfect match. I thought you were different. You seemed so normal, but you're really just a couple of little girls sitting around in your frilly dresses crying 'cuz the other girls were mean to you at the dance.

DANNY. Christ, Emilie!

EMILIE. Gettin' all, "Those bitches better watch out or I'm gonna slam their tits in a locker."

DANNY. I'm so sick of you people throwing the word, you know, the word racist around and then saying shit like that.

EMILIE. "You people." Right. Gotcha. Danny. Last time on this: because your shit and my shit are not the same shit. They are not.

DANNY. Oh my god. You're so smug on the comfy little mountain of your history but that bullshit is the same is the same is the same. Hating is hating, and you may sleep fine at night, but every time I say something that pisses you off, something that hurts you, I toss and turn and I bet you sleep like a fuckin' baby.

EMILIE. That's right.

DANNY. See?

EMILIE. Because Danny, you could go out tomorrow and stick your dick in the first twat you find and the world would suddenly open every single door you think, in your tiny little albino head, is somehow barred to you.

EMILIE. *(cont.)* But no matter what I do, tomorrow is gonna be like today for me. And I love my fucking life, so don't think I'm in some poor-me contest with you. But I am genetically, you know, required to be aware of the world around me. Because I didn't make that fucking world, I just live in it, every day.

PETE. Pretty mouth she has.

TREVOR. Pete I'm gonna–

DANNY. So easy.

EMILIE. Excuse me?

DANNY. To sit there and say that shit, because you don't have to take any, you know, ownership of your words, because you can always fall back on,

EMILIE. What world do you–?

Are you high?

"It was worse for my mom, it was worse for my great uncle, it was worse for everybody else, so, by extension, it's bad for me." But the world is spinning in a slightly forward direction, Emilie.

Bullshit!

And that kind of pain, it's a baton, and it gets passed, you know? You don't get the whole market on oppression forever because some bullshit cracker fuckwads had a labor shortage three hundred fucking years ago. Other people got the pain now. Wake up.

EMILIE. I'm in serious danger of hitting you, Danny.

DANNY. Please. I'd love the excuse.

EMILIE. I don't want to have this with you, you know? This, whatever, this shit, this bullshit with you. Like Trevor said, I can't win this. You can't win this. So let's not, OK? OK? OK, Danny?

DANNY. I'm so… fuck!… so sick of this.

TREVOR. Danny…

DANNY. It's not enough you people take over every theatre in this country one slot at a time–

PETE. Oh, shit.

DANNY. Not enough that you get your government-granted slot of free theatre that takes 15, 20 percent of every theatre's season. February rolls around and the entire nation shuts down for twenty-eight days of liberal hand-wringing. Is there a month for me? I want *my* fuckin' February!

EMILIE. You are so far over the–

DANNY. And it's not enought that the system is set up to heap awards and opportunity on every second-class piece of writing because the author has one name, or a dash or apostrophe in his last name. Where do you think I got that bullshit name for this fucking play? Shaleeha G'natamobi? Good Christ. It's not enough that a guy like me can't even get his play on somebody's fucking pile because it isn't about a crack mother or the birth of blues music or some bus ride in the '60's.

DANNY. (cont.) No. No. No, it's not enough that we have invented an entire system of casting, so that Mrs. Bob Fucking Cratchitt is black or yellow or what have you in every production of *A Christmas Carol* and the kids are like The Reading Fucking Rainbow and nobody can say, nobody can say, "Um, that seems kind of unlikely." It's not enough. It's not enough that you or your cousin or your whatever, direct relation, could write whatever shit he wants about some middle-class Nebraskan family and all it has to do is say "by Jackson J. McBlackman" and people start a bidding war to produce it. It's not fucking enough. No wonder I did what I did here. I'm the new underclass, Emilie.

EMILIE. This is exactly–

TREVOR. You need to stop–

Me. So, yeah, I'll sue you, but I'm fucked because you have my play now, and I'd almost rather people see it than get credit for it, and you had to know that, on some level, you had to know that or you would never have done what you did.

TREVOR. Danny–

TREVOR. All right. We're leaving.

EMILIE. You know what I can't get over?

TREVOR. Let's go.

EMILIE. No way. You know what amazes me? Because on a certain level, some place in me, I get it, Danny, I get it. I get this mentality you have. I hear you. Because all of that must be frustrating. Really. But what stops me is that you can spout such bullshit within a blink of saying how sympathetic you are, how we're the same.

EMILIE. *(cont.)* It's such a fuckin' load that I wish... Maybe it's the gay thing, right? Maybe it's the fact that you've either spent so much time on your knees or facing the headboard that you literally can't keep anything straight. Get it? Can't keep anything *straight*? It's such bullshit that you can spend your time, and maybe this is both of you, maybe it's all of you, I don't know, I'm certainly not going to stoop to some "you people" kind of statement, not like you did, I'm just not built that

DANNY. Here we go.

DANNY. Jesus...

DANNY. "All of you?" All of you.

PETE. Danny, just...

EMILIE. *(cont.)* way. But it's fucking ridiculous that you can look at the world and identify all the places where you think people are less than you because they can't understand your whatever, your fucking pain, even if they've been through some of the same waters. And not just because those theatres you're so mad at, those places that, whatever you said, just give away some percentage of their season to, you know, to… us. Yeah, us. Well, they are all run by fucking gay men. All of them.

TREVOR. Em, please…

DANNY. I didn't say–

DANNY. Not all–

EMILIE. Fucking most of them. Gay men taking away your, Jesus, your precious birthright and handing it over to all those awful, talent-free black folk. Makes your whole point seem a little… what's the word? Gay.

EMILIE. *(cont.)* And you're right, I don't know what high school was like for you, I don't know what it was like to be last on the bench for dodge ball or whatever. What it was like, what it must've been like to not be able to choose between Maria and Anita for who you'd most like to be in fuckin' *West Side Story.*

DANNY. *This* is my– This–

I never said–

TREVOR. Emilie, please.

EMILIE. Oh, no, I know, that's not what you said. You're much more worried about how awful it was that some Equal Opportunity history teacher spent a few too many days on how hard life was on a plantation for your sweet little palate.

EMILIE. *(cont.)* That must have really, really sucked. I get it. But the time for me to sit still and take your bullshit pie like dessert is done now.

DANNY. You're such a hypo–

PETE. Wow, she talks just like you.

EMILIE. Done. So, I'm sorry I took your fuckin' play away from me, but I'm starting to think it wasn't yours to begin with. You may have written it, but given your dirty little mouth, I probably saved you a ton of embarrassment by talking tonight. Because you would've stuck your fat foot in that dirty hole and the thing would be back in a drawer. You should thank me, Danny. Because my guess is this fuckin' play is all you got. And the big sick irony is, in the end, you may have written one good thing, but you still needed a black woman to get anybody to pay attention.

DANNY. You fuckin' bitch.

EMILIE. There we go.

TREVOR. That's it.

(TREVOR starts to go for DANNY. DANNY sidesteps him and TREVOR slips, crashing to the ground.)

Motherfucker.

(He gets up and heads for DANNY again, but EMILIE gets in-between them.)

EMILIE. Stop it!

TREVOR. Let me go!

EMILIE. Trevor!

TREVOR. Emilie, let me the fuck go!

EMILIE. He's not worth it.

(TREVOR pushes away from EMILIE with a great cry.)

TREVOR. FUCK!!!

EMILIE. He's not.

DANNY. Trev–

TREVOR. Fuck off, Danny. Fuck off.

DANNY. *(to* EMILIE, *picking up the script)* Take it all with you, why don't you? Him, this, all of it.

(He hurls the script in EMILIE*'s/*TREVOR*'s direction. The pages go everywhere.)*

Fuck you. Fuck you. Fuck you.

EMILIE. You too, Danny.

DANNY. Just get the fuck out of here. Get the fuck out!

EMILIE. Good. Great. Good.

*(*EMILIE *heads for the door.)*

DANNY. I'll call them, you know. I've got, like, computer files. Dated drafts. All that shit. This isn't hard to fucking prove.

EMILIE. Of course it's not, Danny! I'm not a fucking idiot!

DANNY. So whether you planned it or not, I'm getting it back.

EMILIE. FINE! But what are you getting back? Huh?

DANNY. MY GODDAMN PLAY!

EMILIE. So get it! I never wanted it!

DANNY. Coulda fooled me.

EMILIE. Fuck off, Danny.

DANNY. *(imitating her)* "Fuck off, Danny."

EMILIE. You're seven years old. You're a fucking child, Danny. All y'all got a fuck-all way of talking, no, of thinking, fuck, no, of living. Your bullshit pansy view of things you know not one single thing about makes me wanna, you know, literally vomit. Pushing on me with whatever girly little push you got. You're just another prissy–

DANNY. No room, Em. You got no room here. Bringing your shit to my door.

Pansy? Do you listen when you talk? Do you even fucking– Your lips just flap, they just... You need to get the fuck out of here, you need to take your bullshit out, you, you thief–

EMILIE. queerball–

DANNY. cunt–

EMILIE. faggot!

(*Beat.*)

DANNY. Nigger!

(*Pause. There is a long, long moment of all four stopped by what has just been said.* **DANNY** *and* **EMILIE** *are staring at each other,* **PETE** *and* **TREVOR** *stunned and frozen. Finally, long after this has ceased to be comfortable,* **EMILIE** *starts to laugh. Maybe. Maybe she doesn't. Either way, she pulls herself together before speaking.*)

EMILIE. You know what, Danny? You may be a waste of breath as a human being, but as a writer, you got at least one thing right. It *is* important to know what you're capable of. You know?

(*She walks out the door, letting it shut behind her.* **TREVOR** *starts to leave, but stops at the door.*)

TREVOR. She told them, OK?

PETE. What?

TREVOR. She told them all about it as soon as she left the stage. Hope it's no problem, she gave them your number.

PETE. Why didn't you–

TREVOR. She told me to listen to him.

DANNY. Trev...

TREVOR. Fuck off, Danny.

(*He leaves.* **DANNY** *shakily sits on the couch. There is silence for a moment, and then his cell phone rings.* **DANNY** *doesn't move. After the second ring,* **PETE** *goes to it and answers it.*)

PETE. Hello? No. No, this isn't... What? Yes. Hold on.

(**PETE** *holds the phone out to* **DANNY**)

Babe. Danny. It's–

(**DANNY** *doesn't respond. Beat.* **PETE** *puts the phone back to his ear.*)

PETE. He's not here right now. Yeah. Sorry.

(PETE *hangs up the phone. He crosses over to the couch and sits next to* DANNY. *Beat. The phone in the hotel room begins to ring. After four or five rings,* PETE *gets up to answer it.*)

DANNY. Don't.

PETE. Danny…

DANNY. Don't.

(PETE *looks at* DANNY *for a moment and the phone stops ringing. Beat.*)

PETE. Baby. You can't… I get it. OK? It's… I get it. But the picture is bigger than this, than her, than… You just have to… We're gonna fix this. OK? I love you. You know I–

(DANNY *gathers the pages from the script and slowly starts ripping them up*)

PETE. Hey. Oh, hey. What are you–

(PETE *tries to take the pages back from* DANNY, *but* DANNY *holds onto them.*)

DANNY. Stop it.

PETE. Danny…

DANNY. This is mine.

(DANNY *starts to slowly rip pages again*)

PETE. Baby, come here. I love you so much. Come here. I'm going to make it better, OK? Just let me–

(PETE *goes to touch* DANNY. DANNY *pushes* PETE *away, hard.*)

DANNY. This is what I made.

(DANNY *keeps ripping. Beat.*)

PETE. OK. OK.

(*Long beat. The room phone starts to ring again. Then the cell phone adds in. After five or six rings,* PETE *walks out of the room, leaving* **DANNY** *alone, tearing up his play. The phones continue to ring. And ring. And ring.)*

(Blackout.)

Scene 11

(A Coffee Chain)

(It is six months later. September. Jackets, sweaters. **DANNY** *is sitting, nursing a coffee cup, his laptop closed on his lap, staring dully ahead. He is lost. Beat.* **TREVOR** *crosses, to-go coffee in his hand.* **DANNY** *looks up, they see each other and* **TREVOR** *stops. Beat.* **TREVOR** *crosses to* **DANNY**'s *table.)*

TREVOR. Hi.

DANNY. Um…

   (Beat.)

   Hi.

   (Beat.)

TREVOR. How's things?

DANNY. Um… you know. Good.

TREVOR. Yeah?

DANNY. Sure.

TREVOR. You?

DANNY. What?

TREVOR. You good?

DANNY. Um… you just asked me that.

TREVOR. Oh.

DANNY. How about you?

TREVOR. Oh, good. Fine. Hey, I booked that thing at–

DANNY. Yeah, I heard, the–

TREVOR Yeah.

DANNY. That's…

TREVOR. Yeah…

(Beat.)

DANNY. So… How's–

TREVOR. She's great, Danny.

DANNY. You guys're…

TREVOR. We're great.

DANNY. Good.

TREVOR. Yeah.

DANNY. Yeah.

(Beat.)

I read the interview. The interviews. That was… weird. She comes off kind of…

TREVOR. Danny…

DANNY. No, I mean, she did a good job. I guess. It's OK. It's been a long… It's all kind of numb now, you know? It feels like another life, it seems…

TREVOR. Gotcha.

DANNY. It's just–

TREVOR. OK.

DANNY. Trev, is she writing something?

(Beat.)

Is she?

TREVOR. Yeah.

DANNY. Oh.

TREVOR. Danny…

DANNY. No, no, that's… I was just–

TREVOR. She–

DANNY. Hey. No big deal.

TREVOR. OK.

DANNY. Really.

TREVOR. OK.

(Beat.)

What about you?

DANNY. What about me?

TREVOR. Are you...

DANNY. Oh, I'm... just... waiting for a, you know, an idea to...

TREVOR. Yeah.

(Beat.)

Well, when one does, I'd love to read it when you're...

(Beat.)

Shit. Sorry, I just...

DANNY. Don't worry about it.

(Beat.)

TREVOR. Look, this is probably not the... but...

DANNY. What?

TREVOR. I bumped into Pete last night.

DANNY. Oh.

TREVOR. He's... Danny, he's still so–

DANNY. Please, I–

TREVOR. Can't you just call him? Can't you just–

DANNY. Jesus, Trevor.

(Beat.)

OK?

TREVOR. OK.

(Beat.)

So... I gotta...

DANNY. Yeah. Yeah.

TREVOR. Bye.

*(**TREVOR** starts to go. **DANNY** stares ahead. **TREVOR** stops and watches **DANNY** from behind for a moment before speaking.)*

I think you should just admit you wrote it, Danny. Everybody believes her. People wanna do it here. You know that, I know you know that. You can't say no forever. It's gonna happen. You can only put it off so...

You just gotta... You have to let them, Danny. People wanna see it. It's gonna... You're gonna have to eventually. Make it now. Let them put your name on it. Let them do it. It isn't worth this. It isn't.

(Beat.)

DANNY. OK, Trev.

TREVOR. OK.

(Beat.)

I... you know... I miss you, Danny.

(Beat.)

DANNY. Yeah. Me too.

(Beat.)

All right.

(Beat.)

TREVOR. See you.

DANNY. Hey. Seriously. Tell Emilie I... Tell her I...

TREVOR. I will. Bye, Danny.

DANNY. Bye.

*(**TREVOR** leaves. **DANNY** sits, on the verge of losing it. Beat. His cell phone rings.)*

Hello? Oh, hi. Um... Not great, I... Tonight? No, I... OK, I guess, sure. No, no, let's go out, my place is a disaster... You choose. Whatever you want. Whatever. No, I hate that place. The fries are too spicy. Oh my god, no, no, that spongy bread is kinda... How about that... What? No, that's... Don't they all sit in a big circle or whatever, eat with their– Hmm? What kind of... Pakista– You're killin' me, how 'bout something, you know, normal... something... I dunno, American. Shit. That's not what I... Shit. Sorry. You pick. Please? OK? I can't... Yeah. Yeah. OK.

(He hangs up and stares ahead. It all hits him. A wave of emotion burbles out of him. Beat. Then, quietly, almost contemplatively.)

Fuck. Fuck.

(He sits, staring out at nothing. Beat.)

(Blackout.)

(End of play.)

"*The Submission* is bold, brave, provocative, and entertaining."
    – *Theatrescene.net,* Stewart Schulman

"It's a daring piece of writing [and] proves to be a riveting
affair... [a] play that will most likely have audiences talking for
weeks and months to come.
    – *Theatremania.com,* Andy Probst

"[A] sharp, punchy dramedy.
    – *Time Out NY,* David Cote

"Sharp-edged, fast, frequently funny, and extremely
well-realized."
    – *The Village Voice,* Michael Feingold

OTHER TITLES AVAILABLE FROM SAMUEL FRENCH

LARGE ANIMAL GAMES

Steve Yockey

Comedy / 4m, 3f

This incisive, unexpected, and larger than life tale of sex, love, and self delusion tracks the overlapping escapades of a group of friends old enough to know better in love but still naive enough to mess things up anyway, and the man who supplies them with equal parts tough love, lingerie and self awareness. In a series of fluid scenes, Large Animal Games takes a comically skewed and razor-sharp look at modern relationships through a mix of bullfights, big game hunting and intimate apparel.

"Yockey's plays frequently involve the human fascination with violence, self-destruction and other dark impulses, but *Large Animal Games* turns out to be his brightest and most open-hearted work, and even the bittersweet moments retain a generosity of spirit."
– *Creative Loafing*

"the play has a touch of the magical dimension familiar to audiences who saw [Yockey's] *Skin* or *Octopus*, but it operates here in a more lighthearted way, while still nicely augmenting the subtly related themes of animal-lust, competition, self-image and possesion cleverly at work under the frilly, scanty surface."
– *San Francisco Bay Guardian*

"We are all animals, according to Yockey. And as such, we're enslaved by our primal instincts. The characters in *Large Animal Games* all desire intimacy or fulfillment, but they have different - sometimes bizarre - ways of seeking it."
– *East Bay Express*

OTHER TITLES AVAILABLE FROM SAMUEL FRENCH

NELSON

Sam Marks

Drama / 3m / Interior

Nelson is the story of a young man caught between two worlds. By day, he works as a low-level assistant to a film talent agent. By night, Nelson is the camera man for an underground, gang-related videotape series. As the videos become increasingly dangerous and popular, Nelson develops an overwhelming obsession with a C-List actress. Eventually, Nelson's two worlds collide with disturbing, unsettling results. The play is a darkly comic look at the guilt dream of a man trying to find something authentic in a world of two very different kinds of film.

"A funny-creepy play by Sam Marks."
— *The New York Times*

"Marks continues to offer a fresh urban voice. *Nelson* grabs your ear from the outset with its halting staccato street talk, and in the fine office scenes, Nelson's racist boss attacks him with a Mamet-like patter of disdaining sarcasm."
— *Time Out New York*

OTHER TITLES AVAILABLE FROM SAMUEL FRENCH

RACE

David Mamet

Drama / 3m, 1f / Interior

Multiple Award-winning playwright/director David Mamet tackles America's most controversial topic in a provocative new tale of sex, guilt and bold accusations.

Two lawyers find themselves defending a wealthy white executive charged with raping a black woman. When a new legal assistant gets involved in the case, the opinions that boil beneath explode to the surface. When David Mamet turns the spotlight on what we think but can't say, dangerous truths are revealed, and no punches are spared.

"Scapel-edged intelligence!"
– *The New York Times*

"Provocative and profane!"
– NY1

"Mamet is most concerned with the power and treachery of language: a line of dialogue vital to the prosecution case is cynically rewritten by the defense. Mamet's larger contention is that attempts to create a more equal and tolerant society have made race an unsayable word…brilliantly contrives here a moment in which the single most taboo sexual expletive is ignored by an audience which then gasps at the word "black"…Mamet remains American theatre's most urgent five-letter word."
– *The Guardian*

OTHER TITLES AVAILABLE FROM SAMUEL FRENCH

AFTER.

Chad Beckim

Drama / 4m, 2f

When a wrongfully imprisoned man is exonerated by DNA evidence after seventeen years in prison, he is forced to re-assimilate into a cold, foreign world of toothbrush shopping, doggy day care, and a friendship with an anxious young woman with secrets of her own.

"A compassionate portrait of a man struggling with the challenges of socializing…and the anger he still feels for having his youth unjustly destroyed."
– *The New York Times*

"Carefully, and with human detail, explores just how important our formative years are to us. And shows us just how scary the world might look if we they were taken from us with force"
– *New York Theatre Review*

"Human-scale social drama, approached quietly, one foot in front of the other, with compassion and courage"
– Vulture, the culture blog of *New York Magazine*

SAMUEL FRENCH STAFF

Nate Collins
President

Ken Dingledine
Director of Operations,
Vice President

Bruce Lazarus
Executive Director,
General Counsel

Rita Maté
Director of Finance

ACCOUNTING

Lori Thimsen | Director of Licensing Compliance
Nehal Kumar | Senior Accounting Associate
Glenn Halcomb | Royalty Administration
Jessica Zheng | Accounts Receivable
Andy Lian | Accounts Payable
Charlie Sou | Accounting Associate
Joann Mannello | Orders Administrator

BUSINESS AFFAIRS

Caitlin Bartow | Assistant to the Executive Director

CORPORATE COMMUNICATIONS

Abbie Van Nostrand | Director of Corporate
Communications

CUSTOMER SERVICE AND LICENSING

Brad Lohrenz | Director of Licensing Development
Laura Lindson | Licensing Services Manager
Kim Rogers | Theatrical Specialist
Matthew Akers | Theatrical Specialist
Ashley Byrne | Theatrical Specialist
Jennifer Carter | Theatrical Specialist
Annette Storckman | Theatrical Specialist
Dyan Flores | Theatrical Specialist
Sarah Weber | Theatrical Specialist
Nicholas Dawson | Theatrical Specialist
David Kimple | Theatrical Specialist

EDITORIAL

Amy Rose Marsh | Literary Manager
Ben Coleman | Literary Associate

MARKETING

Ryan Pointer | Marketing Manager
Courtney Kochuba | Marketing Associate
Chris Kam | Marketing Associate

PUBLICATIONS AND PRODUCT DEVELOPMENT

Joe Ferreira | Product Development Manager
David Geer | Publications Manager
Charlyn Brea | Publications Associate
Tyler Mullen | Publications Associate
Derek P. Hassler | Musical Products Coordinator
Zachary Orts | Musical Materials Coordinator

OPERATIONS

Casey McLain | Operations Supervisor
Elizabeth Minski | Office Coordinator, Reception
Coryn Carson | Office Coordinator, Reception

SAMUEL FRENCH BOOKSHOP (LOS ANGELES)

Joyce Mehess | Bookstore Manager
Cory DeLair | Bookstore Buyer
Sonya Wallace | Bookstore Associate
Tim Coultas | Bookstore Associate
Alfred Contreras | Shipping & Receiving

LONDON OFFICE

Anne-Marie Ashman | Accounts Assistant
Felicity Barks | Rights & Contracts Associate
Steve Blacker | Bookshop Associate
David Bray | Customer Services Associate
Robert Cooke | Assistant Buyer
Stephanie Dawson | Amateur Licensing Associate
Simon Ellison | Retail Sales Manager
Robert Hamilton | Amateur Licensing Associate
Peter Langdon | Marketing Manager
Louise Mappley | Amateur Licensing Associate
James Nicolau | Despatch Associate
Martin Phillips | Librarian
Panos Panayi | Company Accountant
Zubayed Rahman | Despatch Associate
Steve Sanderson | Royalty Administration Supervisor
Douglas Schatz | Acting Executive Director
Roger Sheppard | I.T. Manager
Debbie Simmons | Licensing Sales Team Leader
Peter Smith | Amateur Licensing Associate
Garry Spratley | Customer Service Manager
David Webster | UK Operations Director
Sarah Wolf | Rights Director

GET THE NAME OF YOUR CAST AND CREW IN PRINT WITH SPECIAL EDITIONS!

Special Editions are a unique, fun way to commemorate your production and RAISE MONEY.

The Samuel French Special Edition is a customized script personalized to *your* production. Your cast and crew list, photos from your production and special thanks will all appear in a Samuel French Acting Edition alongside the original text of the play.

These Special Editions are powerful fundraising tools that can be sold in your lobby or throughout your community in advance.

These books have autograph pages that make them perfect for year book memories, or gifts for relatives unable to attend the show. Family and friends will cherish this one of a kind souvenier.

Everyone will want a copy of these beautiful, personalized scripts!

ORDER YOUR COPIES TODAY!
E-MAIL SPECIALEDITIONS@SAMUELFRENCH.COM
OR CALL US AT 1-866-598-8449!